Forgiveness is the final form of love.

—REINHOLD NIEBUHR

LOVE'S A MYSTERY

Love's a Mystery

in

HAZARDVILLE
CT

BETHANY JOHN &
GAIL KIRKPATRICK

Love's a Mystery is a trademark of Guideposts.

Published by Guideposts
100 Reserve Road, Suite E200
Danbury, CT 06810
Guideposts.org

Scripture references are from the The Holy Bible, King James Version (KJV).

Cover and interior design by Müllerhaus.
Cover illustration by Dan Burr at Illustration Online LLC.
Typeset by Aptara, Inc.

ISBN 978-1-961441-40-8 (hardcover)
ISBN 978-1-961441-41-5 (softcover)
ISBN 978-1-959633-02-0 (epub)

Printed and bound in the United States of America.

The House That Love Built

by

Bethany John

Only when we give joyfully, without hesitation
or thought of gain, can we truly know
what love means.

—LEO BUSCAGLIA

✒ CHAPTER ONE ❧

He healeth the broken in heart, and bindeth up their wounds.
—Psalm 147:3

Hazardville, Connecticut
June 1894

It's quiet.

Emma Cooke had been waiting for this moment for weeks. Looking at the calendar, marking off the days, almost like a child would count down till Christmas. All her lessons had been taught. All her tests had been graded. The recitals were done.

The students she taught at Dixon Academy for Girls had all gone home for the summer.

It's finally quiet.

There was no more giggling or silly gossip or singing hymns off-key. There was no transporting girls to their fitness class or dining room duty to attend. Her schedule was blissfully clear.

It's too quiet.

Emma had thought she would enjoy this day. It was the end of her first year at the prestigious school. The academy was founded to promote a strong sense of self, individual achievement, and the highest moral and spiritual standards in young women. Emma had attended many schools like it when she was a girl. Her father was a music master, a brilliant instructor who played piano, flute, and clarinet. He gave private lessons to girls from wealthy families all over the United States. And at every illustrious school in which he taught, he made sure his contract included the provision that his daughter would be provided an education at that institution.

It was a smart move. He would never have been able to pay for her schooling otherwise.

He had been gone six years now.

Her father had done so much for her. She thought of him whenever she walked into the beautifully appointed music room in the school. She thought of him on Sundays when she sat in church and heard the first notes of a hymn as the organist started to play, for her father had played the organ masterfully as well. She thought of him Saturdays and holidays and every day. She missed him.

Especially today. Most of the teachers who lived at the inn left shortly after the girls. They were off to see their families for the summer holiday. Only she and Mary remained.

Mary was like her. No parents. No one to visit on the holidays. They had both stayed in Hazardville during the Christmas break too. It wasn't so lonely then. They attended church together and went caroling with some locals.

Almost everyone in town worked for Hazard Powder Company. Everyone knew each other. There was a closeness in this town that Emma wasn't used to. Mama had died when Emma was four, lost while giving birth to a brother who also did not live. Her father and she had moved a lot. Going from city to city, from one school to another, never staying more than three or four years in one place. Father always said it was exciting, but a new place meant leaving behind friends they had made, leaving behind familiarity and comfort, and starting afresh each time.

She had wished for this quiet, this stillness, but maybe it didn't suit her. She had been on the move her entire life.

"Emma?" There was a knock at her door. She would recognize Mary's soft voice anywhere.

"Come in," she called, glad for the distraction from her thoughts.

Mary walked in, her pretty, reddish-blond hair piled high on top of her head, a few tendrils escaping and framing her face. Her cheeks were pink. She looked happy.

"I'm sorry to bother you. I know you were looking forward to your quiet time. The girls were very excitable this week."

"Oh no! Don't be sorry. I'm glad to see you. I'm not used to quiet anymore. I almost don't know how to handle it. Please, sit down."

Mary eased into the armchair next to the bed. "It's glorious outside. I've just come from a walk along the river. Forgot my hat. My grandmother would have kicked up a storm if I ever pulled that around her. She is probably in heaven fussing to whatever angel will listen to her. I've never understood why being hatless is such a bad thing. Fresh air and sun are good for the soul. Why would God create such a perfect thing if he wanted us to hide from it? It seems almost sinful to me."

Emma smiled. Her friend was so plainspoken, the Maine accent still slightly gripping her words. It was almost hard to believe that she was the foreign-language teacher and spoke the most beautiful French, Latin, and Italian.

"I should get outside too." Emma stood up and looked out the window. A beautiful sugar maple, its leaves gently dancing in the breeze, greeted her. "Today seems like the perfect day for a picnic." A memory took hold of Emma. "Remember the day we took our afternoon classes outside for lessons? And how that bumblebee landed on Gemma Alexander?"

"Of course I do! She screamed and screamed and *screamed*. She kept boasting about the expensive French perfume her mother had sent her. The bee probably took her for a flower."

"She was a trying little thing at times, but I will miss her." Emma sighed. "I will miss them all." She looked back at Mary, suddenly feeling a wash of melancholy flood over her. "I thought I was looking forward to this time, but I must admit I don't know what I'll do with myself."

"You could come with me to Boston. My cousin works for Harvard. I'm going to meet his soon-to-be wife and her family. I hear they are fancy people. I'll have to remember all the lessons I learned from the ladies here to try and impress them."

"Thank you for the invitation, Mary, but I couldn't intrude on your family time. I know how close you were to your cousin growing up. You should spend time with him and not worry about me."

"But we are family, Emma. We orphaned, unmarried, educated ladies must stick together."

Mary was right. There weren't many women like them. They had both gone to college and earned degrees. The idea of educating women was a dangerous one to some. Most women their age were married with two or three children. It was simply what women did.

Emma's father didn't want that for her.

"I don't want you to be tied down. I want you to have choices."

Her father made sure she learned from the best. She'd had private lessons from some of the world's best math minds.

She was educated. She earned her own wage. She was supporting herself. Emma had recently begun to wonder if her father knew he wasn't going to live to see her become a woman. After all, he had been quite a bit older than her classmates' fathers. She tried not to think about it, because if he had known and he kept it from her and robbed her of all of the extra moments she could squeeze in with him, she would be very angry with him. She didn't want to be angry with her father. So she tried not to think about it.

"We are a family," Emma said to Mary. "I say we go on a family outing to the shops today. We deserve something sweet for all the hard work we put in this year. It's my treat, and I do not want to hear any arguments from you, Mary."

"No arguments from me!" Mary stood up. "I've been dreaming about pudding for days."

"But do grab your hat this time. I would hate to have your grandmother fussing again," she said with a smile.

Mary went to get her hat, and the two of them walked two blocks to where the shops were located. They got delicious custards and chatted with the new shop owner's wife. Hazardville had been a company town for many years, but after the War Between the States, the gunpowder business started declining. Many people moved on, but there were new people in town too. There was a new public school and a large, gorgeous church. There was community here. Emma liked Hazardville and often wondered what her life would have been like if she had grown up in a place like this. Or just one place instead of many.

She and her father had moved from big city to big city. New York. Boston. St. Louis. San Francisco. She didn't have roots. She never realized how much slower life could be until she came to Connecticut.

Of all the places in the world she thought she might end up, Connecticut wasn't one of them. There was a beauty here she hadn't expected, and people were more open about educating young women.

"I'm not sure about the color of this fabric I bought." Mary glanced down at the bag she was carrying. "Do you think it's too much?"

"Of course I don't. Lilac is a beautiful color. I think it will look lovely with your hair."

"I've never liked my hair. Such an in-between color. Not red. Not blond. My mother had dark brown hair. Almost as dark as yours. I've always thought dark hair was so beautiful."

"We all seem to want what we don't have. I've always thought my hair was too dark."

They returned to the inn, chatting about everything and nothing at the same time. It was nice not to have to rush back and prepare for their next lessons or worry about where the girls were supposed to be next. As they approached the steps of the inn, Emma saw a man in a dark suit standing on the porch, a briefcase in one hand, a packet of papers in the other.

"Miss Cooke?" The man looked directly at her, seeming to already know who she was.

Immediately her heart started to beat a little faster. No one ever came looking for her. In fact, most of her life she felt quite invisible. "Yes?" She swallowed and glanced at Mary, who looked just as perplexed. "How can I help you?"

"I'm Collin Reed. I'm with Caldwell and Wickers."

"Caldwell and Wickers," she repeated. "You're a lawyer?"

She knew the name. She'd seen the ornate sign every day when she lived in New York City. The building was across the street from the school she attended until she was fourteen. It was one of the most prestigious firms in the country. Only wealthy clients could afford their services.

"You know our firm?" he asked, brows raised.

"I went to school at Spencer Academy."

He nodded. "We have clients whose daughters attend that school. I have heard fine things about it." The slight smile dropped from his face, and he was all business again. "Is there somewhere we can go to have a conversation? I have important information to relay."

"Maybe I should leave you alone to discuss your business." Mary took a step away, but Emma caught her hand and held on tightly.

"Maybe you shouldn't. I have no secrets from you." Emma looked back at the lawyer in his very dark suit. "Is there a reason, Mr. Reed, that Mary cannot hear what you are about to tell me?"

"No. I'm sure she would learn the news soon after I leave anyway. The whole town will know shortly."

"The whole town?" Emma shook her head. "No one is suing me, surely. I do not have a penny to my name."

"You are not being sued, miss."

Her head spun as she tried to think of a reason such a high-profile attorney would need to see her. "Both of my parents died penniless. I have no other family."

"If we could go somewhere private, I would be happy to tell you why I am here."

"To be perfectly honest with you, sir, I do not think my feet can move to a private place. They are rooted to this spot. Please, tell me."

Mr. Reed glanced at the chairs to his left on the porch. Without a word, Mary guided Emma to sit on one of them and then sat beside her and held her hand.

"I'll get right to the point. Are you familiar with Miss Virginia Prescott?"

"Miss Prescott?" She looked at Mary. "Of course. Everyone knows who she is." She was the richest woman in town. Her huge home on School Street was completed right before Emma arrived in Hazardville. "She is a patron of the school. She is a strong believer in educating girls."

Mr. Reed nodded. "It was the cause she championed the most."

Emma hadn't exchanged more than a few words with the woman. She found her terrifying, but in the way one finds very regal, very wealthy, people terrifying. The woman was impossibly tall, with stark white hair. Her clothing was perfectly fitted to her long, slender frame—and nothing one could ever find in their gunpowder-producing town. Emma imagined the woman taking trips to New York City or even sailing to Paris to find her meticulously made dresses. She was never flashy, never wore bright colors. Emma had only seen her in navy or gray or brown. Those shades might be drab on another woman, but on Miss Prescott they spoke of her sophistication.

"She left a generous portion of her estate to your school. It was very important to her that it succeed."

"Estate?" She looked at Mary and then back to Mr. Reed.

"Regrettably, she has passed away while abroad, after exhausting all possible treatments to battle her illness."

"Oh my," Emma said. "I'm very sad to hear that. I suppose I should have realized something was wrong when she did not attend graduation. She came to every event at the school, and the girls loved to see her. I think many aspired to have her grace." Emma stood up and went forward to shake Mr. Reed's hand. "Thank you for coming to tell me about the gift she left to the school. I know no one is there right now. Everyone is gone for the summer. I'll be sure to inform the headmaster of it. We have to honor Miss Prescott somehow."

"I'm not here to inform the school of her death, Miss Cooke. I'm here to speak to *you*. To discuss what she has left to you."

"To me?" Emma shook her head. "She left me something? I wasn't aware she even knew who I was."

It was Mr. Reed's turn to look confused. "She not only knew who you were, she thought very highly of you." He handed her the packet of papers. "She has left you her house on School Street and its contents. As well as enough money to maintain the home and its staff for as long as you live there."

"Excuse me?"

Emma felt the air leave her lungs. She was never one for histrionics, but she felt as if she had been bowled over. She sat down quickly, her head spinning.

"My goodness!" Mary exclaimed. "That is unbelievable."

It *was* unbelievable. Emma shook her head. She must be dreaming. Hallucinating. "This is an odd joke. I don't understand who would think this is funny."

"It is not a joke, miss." He pointed to the papers in her hands. "I wrote her will myself. She was very specific about what she wanted."

"She must have been losing her senses!" Emma felt panic welling up inside her. "I barely spoke to her. I only met her a few times. Why would she leave her house to me?"

"I assure you that Miss Prescott was perfectly sound when she made this will. Whatever you have done, you greatly impressed her." He pulled three keys out of his pocket and handed them to her. "I am to escort you to your new home. Your staff is awaiting you."

"My staff? I am staff. I can't have staff."

"You'll need to get used to the idea. This inn is no longer your home."

CHAPTER TWO

Hatred stirreth up strifes: but love covereth all sins.
—Proverbs 10:12

"What have you eaten today, sir?" Dr. Wesley Black asked.

Mr. Mercer gave him that mulish look he always gave him. "What have I told you about calling me 'sir'?" Mr. Mercer's English accent hadn't faded one bit, even though the man had lived in Connecticut for close to fifty years.

"I do not care what you have told me. You are my elder, and I will respect you. Now tell me, sir, what have you eaten today?"

"Coffee."

"That is not food."

"The girl you send over here made me some of that cornmeal mush."

"Did you eat it?"

"I wanted bacon." Mr. Mercer sounded like a small child rather than a man close to eighty. Wes found him amusing but kept his expression neutral.

"Bacon upsets your stomach."

"I'm an old man. I should be able to eat what I want!"

"You'll have stew tonight and a custard pie. You will eat every bit of it."

"And if I don't?"

"I'll send the Morris children over here to sing hymns to you." Mr. Mercer's eyes widened at the threat. "The girl has such a unique voice. Her favorite is 'Amazing Grace.' I will ask her to sing it loudly, as you are hard of hearing."

"I'm not hard of hearing!"

"The Morris girl won't believe that. You're the oldest person in the world to her."

"Those children sound like injured animals. And there are so many of them. You wouldn't do that to me. Didn't you have to take an oath that said you would never do harm?"

"Harm? I'm sending precious children to you to comfort you in your later years."

Mr. Mercer folded his arms across his chest. "I'll eat tonight."

"Caroline will tell me if you don't." Wes refilled Mr. Mercer's cup with water and placed it at his bedside. "I will see you tomorrow."

"You don't have to check in with me every day," Mr. Mercer said quietly.

"I know," Wes replied before he took his leave.

He squinted as he left the tiny one-room house that was no bigger than a shed. The sun was so bright it was nearly blinding. The air was warm, and there was a delicate scent of flowers in the air. It was a perfect spring day. Wes wished he could appreciate it more. All winter he had been looking forward to longer days and warmer weather. It could be so cold and dreary in the Northeast. The nights seemed unnecessarily long. And now spring was here, and in just a few short weeks it would be summer, but Wes could summon no joy in that. He felt numb.

His days as a doctor kept him busy, but he often felt as if he was just going through the motions. Except for the ten or so minutes a day he visited with Mr. Mercer. The elderly man was right. Wes didn't have to check in with him every day, but something compelled him to.

He found the man interesting. Unlike most of the people he had grown up with in Newport.

Mr. Mercer was one of the original skilled gunpowder workers brought over from Faversham, England, to expand the mill into the large operation it was today. He was a young man when he arrived in Connecticut, hardly more than a boy, but somehow he survived working in the gunpowder mill for over thirty years. It was dangerous business. A nasty one, really. Not a spark could go near the stuff. The fear of an explosion was never far from anyone's mind. There had been a few, the last major one in 1871. It was the explosion that had taken Mr. Mercer's only son.

It was only a matter of time before it would happen again.

Wes had seen the aftermath of some of the smaller blasts. The thought of a larger one was enough to keep a man awake at night.

When he started his practice here, he wasn't prepared for how busy he would be. There was another doctor in Hazardville, but the man worked directly for the mill and treated only the workers. Wes was the one who delivered babies and patched up children who fell out of trees and took care of the elderly who needed attending. He was so busy with patients, it was overwhelming. He had time for nothing else.

There was nothing else anyway. No wife to come home to. No children of his own to play with. Medicine was his life. Now more so than ever.

But he did need to sleep. A doctor with no sleep was a danger-ous one, so he had brought on another. A young man, right out of training: Dr. Timothy Smith.

Tim was the first person he saw when Wesley returned to his office. It appeared he had just arrived as well.

"Dr. Black." Tim seemed surprised to see him. "I thought you would be taking the afternoon off."

"Why would you think that?" Wes set his medical bag down.

Tim hesitated. "Because usually people take time to grieve when a family member dies."

Word had reached Wes that morning that his Aunt Virginia had passed away. He couldn't say it was unexpected news. He was with her when she learned she had cancer. Then he went with her to New York to seek treatment from one of the best doctors in the world, but in the back of his mind, he knew that if Aunt Virginia was admit-ting to feeling poorly, it was already too late. Still, he'd thought he would have more time with her.

She was the main reason he came to Hazardville to start his own practice. She was his favorite relative. He could never describe her as warm. In fact, she terrified most people, but he found her to be intelligent, with a sharp wit.

She was so unlike his mother, who married a French man and moved out of the country a year after Wes's father died. His mother was so terrified of being alone. But Aunt Virginia had always been alone. No husband or children. Satisfied with her own company. Not willing to compromise her beliefs for anyone. He had admired her for that.

And for always choosing her own path.

She had wanted to spend her remaining time in one of her favorite places. A little island in the Caribbean. There was nothing he could do or say to stop her, so he didn't attempt to. But he couldn't help but think she had spent her final days alone.

There was no use in wishing for things that could never come true, but he wished he had been able to see her once more.

"Aunt Virginia would think I was very foolish if I sat at home all day just because she passed. I have patients to see. There's no need for me to be home."

"It's not foolish to take time," Tim said gently. "You hired me so you could have more of it. But from what I understand, you are just as busy as you were before I came."

"We can serve twice as many people. I don't mind the work."

"Dr. Black, there will come a day when you will be forced to take a break. You should take one before it gets to that. It could be a break you cannot come back from."

Tim's words were jarring. Wes knew firsthand how short life could be, but he didn't want to think about it.

"I have some paperwork to catch up on. If I do not see you before you leave, have a good night." Wes walked into his office and shut the door, not willing to be a part of the conversation anymore.

He was a young, healthy man. His thirtieth birthday was just two months ago. There was no reason for him to slow down.

He sat at his desk and looked out the window, noticing the sugar maple with its leaves rustling in the wind. The afternoon was quickly turning to evening. Caroline, the woman he hired to cook and clean for him, was probably in his kitchen right now, preparing the stew she had told him she was going to make this morning.

He hadn't eaten all day. He had scolded Mr. Mercer for doing the same thing, but his stomach could accept no food. He hadn't been hungry since he heard the news about his aunt.

He would get no more letters from her. Timothy had been right about him working more. He had managed to find work to do every Sunday since Aunt Virginia had left the country and he had lost the one person he visited on his only day off. He didn't want to think about why he did so.

There was a knock at the door that startled him from his thoughts. He looked away from the sugar maple that had captured his attention and picked up a pen.

"Yes?" he called, expecting to see Tim. Instead, he saw a man of middle age in a dark suit standing in his doorway.

Wes stood up. He knew immediately the man wasn't from Hazardville. "Is there an emergency? At the powder mill?"

"No, Doctor. I'm not from the mill. I'm here on behalf of your aunt, Miss Prescott."

"I've already been notified of her death," he said stiffly.

"Yes." The man took a step forward and extended his hand. "My name is Collin Reed. I am the attorney for your aunt's estate. I am here to discuss her will."

"Her will?" Wes was confused. "So soon?" He shook his head. He didn't want to talk about her will. Splitting her things up. It made everything seem so final. But death was final, wasn't it? "I am sure this can wait for another day. I'm a busy man, and I have no need for anything that she has left me."

"Your aunt was very specific in her instructions about how things were to be carried out upon her death. I know she isn't with us anymore, but I still do not wish to cross her. The woman was formidable. Part of me thinks she is still watching to make sure I follow her instructions."

Wes found humor in Mr. Reed's statement, but he could not manage to smile. "Please, have a seat. I would not want to dishonor my aunt's wishes."

Mr. Reed sat in the chair in front of Wes's desk and removed a single sheet of paper from his briefcase. "Your aunt has left you her father's pocket watch and his Bible as well as the racehorses and stables that are located in Saratoga Springs, New York. From what I understand, they are quite valuable."

Wes nodded. His grandfather had been horse crazy. "What about her house?" She had spent so long building it. Everything about it had to be perfect. Every piece of wallpaper, every fixture, every rug. He had thought she was going to drive the team of builders she had hired to the brink. But they all survived, and she ended up with the most beautiful home in town. It was enormous for a single woman. He had silently questioned why she wanted such a large house that seemed more suited for a family. But he never dared ask her. It was none of his business to know why she wanted what she wanted. "Is it to be sold?"

He figured the profits from the sale would go to charity or education. Aunt Virginia may have seemed cold and exacting, but she gave to causes she believed in. Education was her biggest passion.

"The house and the bulk of her estate went to a Miss Emma Cooke."

This news jolted Wes. "Who?"

"Emma Cooke. She is the mathematics teacher at the Dixon Academy for Girls."

"She gifted the house to the school, you mean?"

"No. She gave a sizeable gift to the school, but the house and the funds to keep it operational all went to Miss Cooke. I gave her the keys an hour ago."

"I am my aunt's closest relative. I have never once heard her mention a Miss Cooke. Why would she leave her home to her?"

"I did not ask your aunt that question. My job was to do as I was instructed."

"Clearly there must be a mistake." Wes's voice grew louder, and suddenly the numbness that had been clinging to him all day fell off. "My aunt could not possibly have been of sound mind when she decided that."

"Dr. Black, I assure you that your aunt was the sharpest woman I have ever known. There was no mistake. Everything she did, she did for a reason. If she did not inform you of her reason, it is because she did not want you to know."

The lawyer was correct. Every letter Aunt Virginia had sent to him in her final days was as eloquent as ever. She hadn't lost her mind, so there had to be another reason she gave her most prized possession to a stranger.

He was going to learn what that reason was if it was the last thing he did.

⚘ Chapter Three ⚘

A man's gift maketh room for him, and
bringeth him before great men.
—Proverbs 18:16

"This is incredible," Mary whispered in awe.

Emma stood in the formal living room of the house, afraid to touch anything. The set of keys Mr. Reed had given her were still clutched in her hand.

She had been to the house once before, when Miss Prescott invited the remaining teachers there for Christmas. But then it was a lark. She had quietly giggled with Mary and the other teachers, whispering about all the ornate details of the home.

The teachers at the school were used to being around wealth. They educated girls from some of the richest families in the United States. Emma herself had been educated with them, but even though she had been taught manners and the basics of mingling with polite society, she knew she was an outsider. There were uniformed servants at the Christmas luncheon, holding trays of Christmas punch in beautiful glasses and passing out French delicacies prepared by a hired chef before they sat down to a feast. Emma had been painfully aware that she and her fellow teachers could never be part of Miss Prescott's social circle.

At the time, Emma wondered why Miss Prescott would invite them to such an event.

Now she was faced with a more confusing question. Why would Miss Prescott leave her this house?

"This has to be a mistake," Emma said. "I clearly don't belong here. I'm half expecting Miss Prescott to walk through the door and have me arrested for trespassing."

"You saw the papers, Emma. You must have done something to leave an impression on the woman."

"I haven't. I haven't done more than you or any other teacher at the school."

Mary walked to the piano. "You played for her at Christmas. She asked you to. She knew you played beautifully, and even I did not know that. When you sang, it must have moved her. I remember I couldn't keep the tears from my eyes."

"Oh, you are too generous with me, Mary. I'm technically proficient. I'm nothing compared to my father." She tried to brush off Mary's explanation, but it was odd that Miss Prescott had singled her out to play that day. Yes, she played in school but just for herself, after the girls were done with lessons for the day and it was just her alone in the music room. She didn't do it often. Only when she was missing her father more than usual.

How could Miss Prescott have known about her playing? She had asked her to sing "O Holy Night," which was Emma's father's favorite Christmas song.

"You are not generous enough with yourself. God has given you gifts. You must deserve them."

"Excuse me, ma'am?" said a woman's voice. Both Emma and Mary turned to look at the doorway. There stood a man and woman. "I'm Caroline, and this is my husband, John. If it is agreeable to you, if you want to keep us on your staff, I will do your cooking and cleaning. John has been taking care of the grounds and the rest of the house since Miss Prescott moved in. I'm good with hair and can help you dress in the morning if you wish."

Emma walked over and extended her hand to Caroline, who seemed shocked at first but returned the gesture. "I'm Emma. This is my friend Mary. It's lovely to meet you both, but I think there has been a mistake. This can't be my house."

"But it is, ma'am. Miss Prescott sent a letter. She said to get the house ready for its new owner and that we would be able to stay and work for you if you so desired."

"Please call me Emma," she said, feeling uncomfortable.

"We won't be doing that, ma'am." John spoke for the first time. "Miss Prescott put your name in the letter. She did not make mistakes. We are hoping we now work for you."

"But I didn't know the woman! Did she say why she left me her home?"

"No, ma'am." John shook his head. "What Miss Prescott says is what happens. We don't question it. We wouldn't think of it."

Emma didn't know how to respond to that. It was just as well, because a man wearing a thunderous expression on his face came storming into the room.

"Dr. Black!" Caroline exclaimed. "I promise I didn't forget about your supper. I have my eldest, Jenny, watching the stew at your house."

"I'm not here about supper. I'm here to see the con artist my aunt left her most prized possession to."

"Con artist!" both Emma and Mary said at the same time.

Dr. Black advanced toward them. "Which one of you is it? Which one of you conned my aunt out of her house?"

"Dr. Black," John said, "I've never known you to be rude to ladies. I would expect your aunt would be very disapproving if she heard how you were speaking to them now."

Emma expected the doctor to have a sharp reply. John worked for his aunt. Surely he had no place correcting not only his employer's nephew but one of the most well-respected men in town. To her surprise, Dr. Black took a breath, and the hot anger in his face faded out.

"Forgive me," he said. "You are correct. I have forgotten myself."

Emma recognized the doctor. She had seen him around town before. He always seemed incredibly busy, rushing from one place to another. He was hard to miss. He was tall, over six feet, with dark brown hair and sharp, dark eyes.

The only time she had seen the doctor more than just in passing was at the Christmas luncheon. It was a happy occasion for them all, but Emma had not once seen the doctor smile that day—or any other time for that matter.

She hadn't heard much about the man except that he was very good at what he did and that he was unmarried. The connection to Miss Prescott wasn't what people spoke of when they spoke of him.

Hazardville was a kind town with good people, but there was gossip here just like every place else. However, there was never any gossip about Dr. Wesley Black.

He was their doctor. He delivered their babies. He sat with dying patients.

He was respected.

And now he was in front of her with a hard look in his eye, accusing her of being a con artist.

"Forgive me," he repeated, looking at Mary first and then at her.

"I am Emma Cooke," she said firmly. "The woman you are accusing of conning your aunt."

Wes had seen this woman before. He couldn't remember the exact places besides his aunt's home at Christmas last year. But he had admired her every time he'd seen her. She was beautiful—not in the generic way that many well-bred ladies were, but she was striking. She was taller than average, her forehead coming up to his chin. She had the figure of a woman who looked like she ate a sweet or two and enjoyed them. Her hair was so dark that it was almost black, and her skin had beautiful olive undertones.

She didn't look like a schoolteacher, even though she was dressed like one. Before Christmas, he might have been able to forget her, but he had heard her sing.

He remembered that day clearly. It wasn't out of character for his aunt to host some sort of party during the holidays. Usually, she held it in Hartford, where she lived most of the time. There she would invite all the Connecticut elite. Politicians, tycoons, socialites. Wes avoided those parties. But when she told him that she was hosting a party in Hazardville, he was surprised and intrigued. Part of him wanted to decline the invitation, but a bigger part was curious to see how the locals would interact with his aunt. For the most part, they were relaxed and plainspoken, with just a few so awestruck they seemed unable to put a sentence together when they were introduced to their hostess.

He snuck away to the kitchen when he heard someone suggest they sing Christmas carols. John was there. Technically, the man was his aunt's employee, but Wes thought of him as somewhat of a friend. As much of a friend as he'd had since he moved to Hazardville.

John poured him something to drink, and they sat across the table from one another. John wasn't one for small talk, and neither was he. Wes much preferred the quiet of the kitchen to the fuss of the party.

But then he heard the piano and, unlike the earlier music, this was more masterfully played. He didn't recognize the tune until he heard her singing.

O Holy Night.

It wasn't the voice of a warbly soprano. It was rich. It was full. It was enough to make him get to his feet to see the person it was coming from.

It had been coming from the woman standing before him now.

She looked him directly in the eye, her own filled with fire.

"I beg your pardon, Miss Cooke," Wes said. "My aunt had few relatives. I was closer to her than anyone else. I have never heard her mention you."

"I did not know your aunt, Doctor. Her leaving me this house is just as much a surprise to me as it obviously is to you."

"She almost fainted when she heard the news," the other woman said. She was dressed similarly to Miss Cooke. He assumed she was another teacher. "She told the lawyer a dozen times that he had the wrong person."

Miss Cooke nodded. "I thought there must be a mistake. I did not know your aunt well, and I certainly did not con her out of her house."

"My aunt never made mistakes."

"So I've been told," Miss Cooke said.

"My aunt was no fool. She just wouldn't give you her house for no reason."

"So you are accusing me of stealing it?"

"According to her attorney, the house appears to be yours legally. But there is much more to this story, and I intend to find out what it is. If I discover that you have done anything to harm my aunt, I will make sure you are prosecuted to the fullest extent of the law."

Miss Cooke's eyes flashed with anger, and Wes found her even more beautiful than he had when he first saw her. The feeling shook him. This entire day shook him. He turned away and left the house.

He needed to think, and he clearly couldn't around her.

CHAPTER FOUR

For I reckon that the sufferings of this present time are not worthy
to be compared with the glory which shall be revealed in us.
—Romans 8:18

Emma had slept at the inn last night. Even though Caroline and John had assured her that the house was hers, she didn't feel right staying there.

It must be a mistake.

That was the only thought that circulated in her head during her long, sleepless night.

It was too much. She didn't want the house. She didn't deserve the house.

She got up early and dressed in her nicest dress. She needed to feel her best for what she was about to do. It was the same dress she had worn when she interviewed for her position at the school. She had interviewed with the headmaster and the school's founder. It was a pleasant enough experience, considering that they recruited her from a smaller school. She had also met the board that day. It was a brief meeting. She had been overwhelmed by the whirlwind process. It was her good fortune that the school was searching for a female math teacher. There weren't many like her, college educated and trained specifically in the area of mathematics.

A few of the board members told her that she came highly recommended. Emma guessed it must have been one of her former professors who mentioned her name, but after that day she hadn't thought much about it. That was the first time she had met Miss Prescott.

She could remember the woman critically studying her. Many wealthy people did that. Emma had spent her life just on the edge of high society. Educated with them but never one of them. She was the music master's daughter. Tolerated because of her father's talent and skills. Never accepted. Never good enough to be considered one of them.

It made sense that the doctor was upset and shocked by her inheritance. He was one of them. Old money. Older bloodlines. He had probably expected the house. By all sensible measures it should have gone to him. But even if he didn't want the house, he probably didn't want it to go to a person like her.

She left the inn early, before Mary and most of the other tenants were awake, and walked to Dr. Black's office.

Lord, give me Your strength, she silently prayed over and over as she walked. She couldn't get the doctor's contemptuous expression out of her mind. But she wouldn't back down to him. She wouldn't let him accuse her of something she hadn't done.

The sun was barely over the horizon when she reached his office. She had a feeling he would be there. He seemed like one of those people who never slept. It also might be why he never smiled.

Emma placed her hand on the doorknob and felt her heart start to beat a little faster.

She wasn't sure why nerves rushed her in that moment. He had made her so angry yesterday when he accused her of being a con artist. She had never stolen a thing in her life! But she had had time to process, to see his side of things. What else was he to think? If their situations were reversed, what would she think?

She got up the courage to turn the knob but did not get the chance. The door was pulled open, and a young, handsome man with an almost angelic air about him was before her.

"Good morning, miss. Are you in need of a doctor?"

She had heard that another doctor was hired a while ago. She had also heard from the girls at school that he was quite handsome. One of them even said that she needed to take up fainting so she would have an excuse to see him.

Emma understood why they were so excited about the new hire. He had a boyish quality about him. The exact opposite of his new employer.

"No. I'm fine, thank you. I am here to see Dr. Black. Is he in?"

"I am." She heard his deep voice and looked up to see him standing on the threshold of what looked like an office. He was such a large man. His shoulders took up nearly the entire width of the doorway. "It's okay, Tim. I'll see her."

The young doctor stepped aside and let her in.

"Dr. Timothy Smith, this is Miss Emma Cooke," Dr. Black said. "She is the mathematics teacher at the girls' school."

"The Dixon Academy for Girls." Dr. Smith smiled at her. "A lovely school. I have only been there once, when your stable hand was kicked by a horse."

"That was a very exciting day for all of us," Emma said. "We are grateful for your treatment. Horace has made a full recovery."

"I have never been to your school, Miss Cooke," Dr. Black said, and she was forced to look at him again. He was across the room, and yet his eye contact was direct and steady. It made her cheeks feel hot. "You have a hundred girls in attendance I've heard, and yet there is rarely a call for a doctor."

"We have a nurse on staff. She does a fine job taking care of the girls' needs." Even to her own ears, Emma's words sounded harsh.

"Is the admissions process very difficult?" Dr. Smith asked, causing Emma to break the uncomfortable eye contact and look back at him. "I have a younger sister. I would like for her to be educated there. We don't have the right family connections though, I'm afraid."

"Family connections help some girls. They are not everything for Dixon Academy, however. There is an application process. She would need recommendation letters, but the interview is the most important part. We are looking for young ladies who are independent, inquisitive, and who have a strong moral center. There are plenty of schools for rich girls, but we want our girls to lead rich lives."

"You should put that in the school literature," Dr. Black said dryly. "I'm assuming you aren't here for a social call."

"No." Emma felt her cheeks grow hot again. The man was so pompous. "We do have an important matter to discuss."

Dr. Smith looked back and forth between the two of them, clearly confused about what was going on. Emma was surprised that Dr. Black hadn't smeared her name all over town by now.

"It's fine, Tim. Go on your calls. Miss Cooke." He stepped out of the doorway he was standing in, alerting her that she should come in.

She walked into his office. This wasn't the place he saw patients. This was no exam room. There were dozens and dozens of thick books lining dark mahogany shelves. The walls were painted darker than the room she had just passed through. It was almost cave-like, but the room felt lived in. There was a coffeepot on his desk and a cup that was still full. There was a plate filled with scones and jam, and a ledger lay open on the blotter.

Clearly the doctor spent much of his time in this room. She wondered where he lived. Many doctors worked out of their homes, but Emma got the feeling Dr. Black lived at work.

"I didn't mean to disrupt your breakfast. I can come back later."

"You will not come back later." He produced another cup from a side cabinet. "Please, sit," he said firmly. "How do you take your coffee? Or would you prefer tea? I can boil more water."

"Coffee is fine," she said as she sat down on one of the chairs opposite his desk. Waiting around for water to boil would send her over the edge. "Milk and sugar, please, if you have them."

"I do." He placed a beautiful cream pitcher and sugar bowl on the desk.

"This is lovely," she said more to herself than to him as she picked up the sugar bowl. It was hand-painted, with beautiful abstract flowers in bold reds and blues and greens. It was the most colorful thing in this dark office. It didn't fit him, but it did seem to fit in this space.

"It was a gift from my aunt. She said it's Italian. I think it's a bit much for a coffee set."

"Her taste was impeccable. It's a talent I don't have. I could never go into a room and know what would look good there."

She looked up to find him staring intently at her. Her eyes locked with his, and suddenly she felt like she had been caught doing something wrong.

She put the little bowl down and sat up straight, embarrassed that she had forgotten herself so quickly.

"You're right, my aunt's taste was impeccable."

The most annoying thing about Emma Cooke was that he still found her beautiful. The way she picked up the sugar bowl and held it in her hand, turning it over to study every colorful inch of it. Looking at it with such awe. She gave her attention so fully to it. Wes wondered what it would be like if she paid attention to him like that for a moment. Looked at him with awe.

It was a foolish thought, and he shook himself out of it. What on earth was wrong with him?

"I didn't come here to talk about china. I came here to talk about the house." She took a set of keys out of her pocket and set them on his desk. Two of them looked like typical keys. He had seen those before, but the third one was bigger than the others, more ornate, and appeared to be bronze.

"I understand how painful it must be to lose your aunt. I have no family." She swallowed hard, emotion seeming to shake her. "My father died just before I went to Wesleyan University. The only thing I have left of him is his hymnal." She smiled sadly for a moment. "It was funny. He claimed he was not a religious man. I used to have to beg him to go to church with me every Sunday. But he would always go, and he knew every word to every song in that book. It was the only time he would sing. He was a music master, but his specialty was instruments, mostly piano, but he had the most beautiful voice."

He found himself hanging on her every word, unable to take his eyes away from her for even a moment. There was grief in her voice. He felt her sorrow. He felt her amusement about her father's protest. He felt her love for the man radiate through her.

She was either telling the truth or she was the most talented actress in the world.

Only someone with such talent could con his aunt. He was conned himself, because he didn't want to believe she was capable of such a lie.

He poured her coffee and put two sugar cubes and a healthy amount of cream in it. He didn't ask her if it was too much. It just seemed the way she would like it. He handed it to her. "Tell me more about him."

She looked at her coffee and took a long sip. She closed her eyes briefly, and he watched her swallow the coffee. She was beautiful even just doing that.

"My father loved coffee," she said. "Strong, horribly bitter, black coffee."

"My father did too. He was a man's man, as my grandfather called him. He was also horse crazy, like my grandfather. I guess it made sense for my aunt to leave me his stable and thoroughbred horses. I do not want them though. I've seen too many injuries from the sport of horse racing."

"Maybe you would like the house instead." She slid the keys closer to him. She was back to being all business. "It is what I came here to discuss. I realize it must have been shocking to hear that I was the one who inherited your aunt's home. I also realize that there must have been a mistake. I have no need for such a grand house."

"Would you like a smaller one?"

She seemed put off by the question for a moment. "I would like a home of my own. An actual home and not a rented room. A place that I wouldn't have to move from every few years."

"You've had to move every few years?"

"We moved a lot when I was a child. I've seen more of the country than most. My father's career took us many places."

"But none of them you call home."

"No," she said softly. "I think a little cottage with a garden would suit me nicely."

"Is that all you want?" She had to have bigger dreams.

"That is enough for me. I have been saving as much of my salary as possible. Maybe it will happen one day."

"Is that really all you want?" He pressed her, feeling there was more.

"A husband and a child would be nice but will not make me complete. I am complete the way the Lord has made me. I have my work and the girls at school. I am content."

"You can have more than contentment. You can want more for your life."

He wanted more. Most days he could ignore the feeling, but he wanted more. He wanted more so bad his bones ached, but that was a secret he kept to himself. However, the thoughts had become more and more intrusive after his aunt left for the Caribbean. And now that he knew she was gone for good, the thoughts were so loud, they were screaming.

"I didn't come here to talk about this. I'm trying to give you the house back."

"You cannot give it back to me. It was never mine."

"Fine, then. I am giving it to you for the first time." She huffed in annoyance. "You have an uncanny way for getting me off topic. Take the house. It clearly wasn't meant for me." She stood up. "I have taken too much of your time, Doctor."

"I don't think you can just give me the house. It was willed to you by my aunt, and besides, I don't want it either. I have my own comfortable home."

"You don't want the house? You accused me of conning your aunt out of it!" Wes heard the hurt in her voice, and he felt an unexpected guilt rise in his chest.

"I apologize for my behavior yesterday. I was in shock. I found out my aunt died, and then a few hours later a lawyer is telling me that she gave the bulk of her estate to a woman she barely knew. I think I am well within my rights to want to know why. Wouldn't you be curious?"

"Yes," she admitted. "We find ourselves in similar positions. Both shocked by the news, and it appears that neither one of us wants the house. But, unlike you, I have no attachment to it or its former owner. That is why I am giving it to you so all of this can end. You can sell it or live in it or turn it into an orphanage, but it will be yours, and you can sleep soundly knowing that no con artist has duped your family. More importantly, you and I never have to speak again."

You and I never have to speak again.

The words hit him squarely in the chest.

She turned to leave, but he picked up the keys, walked around his desk, and took hold of her wrist.

He couldn't let her walk out the door just yet.

There was a big part of him that wanted to believe her. He wanted everything to be as simple as she laid it out for him. But none of this was simple. They couldn't pretend like nothing had happened.

The thoughts of her wouldn't vanish from his head in a few days.

She could be a master con artist, a skillful liar. She could be up to nefarious things he couldn't even imagine. Or she could be innocent. She could just be a teacher that his aunt had taken a liking to for some reason.

He needed to know the truth about her. He wouldn't be able to think about anything else until he did.

If she was innocent, then he could let this go with a clear conscience, but if she wasn't... He wasn't sure what he would do if he found out she wasn't.

"Don't you want to know?" he asked her.

"Know what?"

"Don't you want to know why she chose you?"

"Maybe she picked my name out of a hat. Or maybe she decided it would be a grand lark to give her house to one of the teachers at the school she loved. Or maybe she just loved math."

"I can assure you, my aunt had no great love for mathematics."

"I don't know why she gave me her house, but I do not want it. I've lived a quiet life. I had no trouble before this, and I want to return to that."

"You must be curious. You must wonder why."

"Of course I wonder why!" Her eyes went wide. Her voice was too full of emotion for her to be faking. "I couldn't sleep last night thinking about it. I replayed every interaction I have ever had with her in my mind. I thought back on every significant moment in my life and can't think of a single thing I have done to deserve this."

"Then let's find out," he said. "Together. We both want to know the same thing, and neither one of us will be able to find peace until we find the answer."

"How on earth do you suppose we go about doing that? We don't even like each other. How can we work together?"

He wasn't sure what these feelings he was having for her were, but they weren't dislike. He was sure of that.

"Maybe she left clues."

"You are suggesting we go on a wild-goose chase?"

"Yes. Your students are gone. You haven't left town for a holiday. What else do you have to do?"

She was quiet for a long moment. "Nothing. I have nothing else to do. And I probably won't be able to think about anything else until this matter is settled."

"I have patients to see this morning, but I will call on you at the house, and we can discuss it further."

"I'm not staying at the house. I live at the inn. You can call on me there."

"I'll meet you at the house," he said firmly.

"Very well, if you insist. When?"

"I can't give you an exact time. I make my house calls in the afternoon."

Her eyes sparked. "You expect me to sit around all day, waiting for you to grace me with your presence?"

He couldn't put his finger on it, but something about her question reminded him of his aunt. Physically, they were nothing alike. He couldn't even say that they had similar personalities, but there was something. His aunt would also never sit around waiting for anyone.

This woman pushed back. People rarely pushed back with him. He was a doctor, a well-respected man. People did as he asked.

Well, except Mr. Mercer. Maybe that was why he had a fondness for his oldest patient.

"I will try my best to be there by four. If there is an emergency, I will send a note."

She nodded. They looked at each other silently for a long moment, not breaking eye contact. It was then he realized his hand had slipped off her wrist.

Her hand was in his. It was small, soft, much more delicate than his own.

Her skin was warm. He couldn't think of the last time he had held a woman's hand just to hold it. Maybe he never had.

He didn't want to let go.

He didn't want to let go, and because of that he knew he had to.

He dropped her hand a little too quickly. The absence of its warmth was nearly shocking.

What are you doing?

This felt like madness. He couldn't trust her.

He couldn't *like* her.

He pressed the house keys into her hand, feeling the warmth of her skin again, and took a step away from her. "I have a patient coming in soon. I will see you later."

She blinked at him. He saw confusion and then hurt flash in her eyes. "Of course. Forgive me for taking up so much of your time."

She walked out without another word. He didn't watch her go, but he heard the swish of her long skirt and then the front door close.

He wanted to believe she was on the up-and-up. But his thoughts and emotions were at war. She appeared genuine and sincere. Then again, a good con artist mixed truth with their lies. Her offering him the house could possibly be a ploy to throw him off. She had to know that legally she couldn't just give him the house. This could all be a part of her big plan.

He was going to work alongside her, and, one way or another, he would learn the truth. He wouldn't rest until he did. But he had other options to explore toward that end as well. He opened one of his desk drawers. A few months ago, he had placed a business card in there. It belonged to a private investigator out of Hartford. He was the brother of a man he had saved. He had thanked Wes as he handed him his card and told him that he owed him. Wes thought nothing of it at the time, but he kept the card.

This must be the reason he did.

He quickly wrote a note and then left his office in search of a messenger.

He was going to learn everything he could about Miss Emma Cooke.

৩ CHAPTER FIVE ৩

*Only by pride cometh contention: but with
the well advised is wisdom.*
—*Proverbs 13:10*

Emma tried to walk off her annoyance after she left Dr. Black's
office. She thought walking along the banks of the Scantic River
would calm her, but even the peaceful sound of the rushing waters
failed to soothe her. The annoyance stayed with her, burning in her
stomach as she tried to go about her day.

As much as she wished to blame her mood on the doctor, she
had no one to blame but herself. She hadn't known what to expect
when she walked up to his office door that morning. She was so
filled with jittery nerves from her sleepless night that she could
hardly put two sensible thoughts together. But she had hoped when
she returned to the inn she would have some peace. And that this
odd fever dream would end.

Most of all, she had hoped that she wouldn't have to see him
again.

It was the oddest of meetings. The whole interaction was outside of everything she could have expected. She had seen him
around town perhaps a dozen times. No warmth had ever radiated
from her. There was no sign of a personality at all.

Yesterday, he was biting and harsh when he accused her of scamming his aunt.

But today, he was altogether different. It might have been the way he looked at her, like he was taking in every inch of her. She had gone to a women's college. Her coworkers were women. She taught girls. It was rare for her to be in the presence of a man. That might have been why she noticed how broad his shoulders were and the strong cut of his jaw and how the sunlight revealed the lighter streaks of brown in his hair.

It might have been why she thought his deep voice was almost soothing. It might have been why she was so discomfited by the feel of his hand on hers.

He had held her hand, and she froze in place, unable to make her feet go. He was a medical professional. He touched hundreds of people. Surely, the touch meant nothing to him. It didn't make his cheeks grow hot. It didn't make his stomach flutter.

She was no green girl at twenty-four. She was a mathematician. An educator. She hadn't expected to feel that way. She hadn't expected him to ask about her life. She hadn't planned to reveal to him so much about herself in that short meeting.

She had told him about her father. About what she secretly hoped for. She revealed too much of herself, and she was angry about it.

She liked to keep personal things to herself. There were things about her life that others wouldn't understand. She wasn't raised like other women. People judged. They didn't always agree with the way her father raised her.

Dr. Black couldn't be trusted. He had accused her of being a thief. He was warm to her one moment and coldly dismissing the next. She was annoyed with herself for being affected by him.

There was a knock on her door, and she was relieved once again to be distracted from her thoughts. "Come in, Mary."

Mary appeared, looking a little surprised. "How did you know it was me?"

Emma smiled at her. "Who else would be knocking on my door?"

"I've come to see how you are feeling." Mary walked into the room and shut the door behind her. Emma had never been more grateful to have Mary as friend. If she hadn't been there yesterday, Emma wasn't sure how she would have made it through the day.

"I'm feeling too many things," she admitted.

Mary nodded and gave her a sympathetic look. "That's to be expected. Yesterday morning, you were just a teacher. Today you're an heiress."

"An heiress." Emma laughed at the term, but she didn't find the situation funny.

"I thought you might have gone to the house today. You didn't explore it yesterday while you were there."

"It's not my house to explore. I felt odd being in there. Like I sneaked into someone else's home."

"But you didn't sneak in. There was a will and a lawyer who came with the will to prove it is now your home. You have every right to be there."

Emma buried her face in her hands. "I never want to see that house again."

"Why not? It is the most beautiful house I have ever seen. I grew up on a farm. That is a dream home."

"Do you want it? I'll give it to you." She looked up at Mary. "Then you can deal with the world's most infuriating, pompous doctor."

"Emma." Mary sat next to her and patted her hand. "I know how it must have upset you when he accused you of conning his aunt, but anyone who knows you can attest to the fact that you didn't know her any better than anyone else at the school. We all know that you are a good person. Don't let the doctor intimidate you."

"I went to his office this morning and offered to give him back the house."

"Oh, why would you?" she exclaimed. "Besides, you cannot give something back that was never his in the first place."

"That is what he said. It was the most infuriating conversation. He says he doesn't want the house. He simply wants to know why his aunt left it to me."

"Well, that makes two of you. You are curious, aren't you?"

"I am. But there could be no reason at all. It could have been a whim."

Mary shook her head. "I don't believe it was a whim. Everything happens for a reason, and the Lord works in mysterious ways. I believe that God has blessed you with this house. It is wrong to refuse a gift from God."

"I'm not refusing it. I just believe that this gift was meant for someone else."

"You should treat it like it is yours until you learn otherwise. Sleep in the grand bedroom. Let Caroline cook you a delicious dinner."

"But what if it is all a mistake?"

"Then you go back to living here and go on with your life as it was. You can think of this as a vacation. When else are you going to have this opportunity? Women like us never get to see how the other half lives. Do it for all the girls who grew up poor. Do it for all the girls who were told that educating them would be worthless. Do it for me. I could use a vicarious adventure."

Emma was silent for a moment, thinking about Mary's words. She was right. What harm could there be in staying in the house for a little while till things were settled? It could be a story she would tell her children one day. "Thank you, Mary." She lifted her chin. "I'm going to take your advice."

"I'm glad." She patted Emma's hand.

"Now go pack a bag."

"Pack a bag?" Mary's eyes went wide.

"Yes. You don't think I'm going to stay in that house alone, do you?"

Wes arrived at his aunt's home a few minutes after four. Usually, he went through his house calls almost mechanically. He asked the same questions of his patients, administered medication, and spoke to family members. It had been a while since there was a true emergency. Most days there wasn't anything to get his heart pumping. He would finish his calls, go back to his office for a few hours to complete his paperwork or see any unexpected patients who dropped by, and return to his quiet little home behind his practice and eat whatever meal Caroline prepared for him. Then he would read for a few hours before he drifted off into a dreamless sleep. After his aunt left the country, there was no one to visit socially. His days blended together, one nearly indistinguishable from the next. His house seemed emptier than ever.

He had briefly entertained the idea of finding a wife. But Hazardville wasn't a big city. There weren't many social occasions to meet women, and besides, most of the single women who were of marrying age seemed so dreadfully young to him. Barely out of the schoolroom. What could he possibly have in common with them?

But then again, did he need to have anything in common with them? He wanted a wife so he wouldn't come back to an empty house. He wanted a wife to give him children so he could pass on his family name.

But the idea of spending the rest of his days with someone he couldn't talk to sounded dreadful, so he never gave it more than a passing thought.

It was funny that the thought had passed through his mind today. It was also odd that for the first time in a long time he went through his day feeling more like a man than a machine. He knew that when he finished his calls there would be something different waiting for him.

Could it be that he was looking forward to seeing the mysterious Miss Cooke again?

The door opened, and it was John standing on the other side.

"Dr. Black, come in. Miss Cooke is expecting you."

"Why are you being formal? You call me Wes. We are friends."

John grinned. "As your friend, then, I am warning you to watch your tone with Miss Cooke today."

He respected John for his warning. "I will. I have apologized to her already."

"She's very kind. She went to the shop in town and brought back sweets to thank us. Can you believe that? We work for her."

We'll see how long that lasts, he thought to himself, and then he felt guilty for it. "What do you know about her?"

"Not much," John said. "I've seen her in church from time to time. She usually sits in the back. Doesn't linger after the service. She mostly keeps with the other teachers at the school."

"You have never seen her with my aunt before? She's never come to the house? Made an unexpected visit?"

"The only time I have seen her here was last Christmas. Caroline was there more. Maybe she will have a different answer for you, but I doubt it."

John went off to finish his work, and Wes headed to the kitchen, where not only Caroline but Miss Cooke and her friend were as well. Caroline was standing over the stove, and the other two women were at the counter, their hands filled with dough, their faces smudged with flour. Both were laughing, but his eyes rested on Miss Cooke. It was entirely maddening how beautiful he found her with her hair escaping its pins and her cheeks pink with delight.

"Good afternoon, ladies," he said, making his presence known. Miss Cooke's smile dimmed when she set her eyes upon him.

"Good afternoon, Dr. Black. We are making bread." She sounded slightly defensive.

"I see. That is something I'm sure my aunt never did."

"We don't have access to the kitchen at the inn," Miss Cooke explained. "We got excited when we saw the oven and begged Caroline to let us help her bake."

"Can you imagine such a thing, Dr. Black? These educated ladies begging me to let them cook. Miss Cooke owns the house. She can help me in the kitchen any day she pleases."

"I don't know anything about the culinary arts," Miss Cooke admitted. "Mary does though. She has told me many stories of the things she used to eat growing up in Maine. I'm hoping we get to try them all now."

"You will be using the kitchen here?" he questioned.

"Yes," she said, lifting her chin. "The house is legally mine, even if just for a little while. It shouldn't sit empty. This house was meant to be filled with people."

Wes had thought that himself on many occasions after his aunt built it. Out front was a large wraparound porch that begged to be sat on. The house had six bedrooms to his knowledge, but he had yet to see them all. There was also a formal parlor, an informal sitting room, and a dining room that was large enough to hold at least twenty guests. The house was three stories, painted blue and white, and had a turret to top it all off. It was the crown jewel of this working-class town. He had worried about his aunt being here all alone. That was why he had come to visit her so often. She never appeared lonely or in need of company, however. She sometimes had dinner guests to fill her evenings. Other times she wouldn't be here at all. He would learn from John or Caroline that she was off to Hartford or Boston or anywhere in between, visiting her friends.

"You aren't staying here alone, are you?" He had never been worried about his aunt's safety, but for some reason the thought of Miss Cooke sleeping here alone bothered him.

"Hazardville is the safest place I have ever lived. I am not worried about my safety here." She smiled. "However, I have invited Miss Mary Dutton to stay with me. This house is very large."

"I am Miss Dutton, by the way," the other woman said as she waved. "I'm sure you must have figured that out by now. We haven't been formally introduced."

"Hello, Miss Dutton. I am glad to make your acquaintance. I'm assuming you are also a teacher."

"I teach foreign language. Mostly French, but I do have a few advanced pupils who are learning Latin."

"I learned Latin. I found it to be useful in medicine but not much else."

"I'm assuming you don't have much use for French either," Miss Dutton said, grinning.

He shook his head. "My mother married a Frenchman and currently lives in France. Perhaps if I get the burning desire to communicate with my stepfather, I will call upon your expertise."

"Do sit down, Dr. Black," Miss Cooke said. "You might as well join us for dinner. It will save Caroline a trip to your house later."

He nodded and took a seat at the kitchen table.

"Can I offer you something to drink?" Miss Cooke wiped her hands on her apron. "There is lemonade. Or maybe you would prefer…something stronger?" She stumbled on the question. "I'm sure there must be something of the sort in a house this grand."

"Something stronger?" He found himself smiling at her attempt to make him comfortable. She was quite adorable with her flour-smudged face and her innocent question. "My aunt didn't approve of the consumption of spirits, and I can tell by your question, neither do you."

"Oh." Her cheeks went pink. "I did not mean to sound judgmental."

"You didn't. At any rate, I do not drink alcohol. Lemonade will be fine."

She went to the icebox and pulled out a pitcher. She seemed perfectly comfortable in the kitchen. It was a sign that she had not grown up with servants as he had. His mother had never lifted a finger. Yet it was a step down from how she used to live before she married Wes's father. She and Aunt Virginia grew up extremely wealthy in Newport with an army of servants. Their massive childhood home was a mansion that overlooked the ocean.

Wes's father was only moderately wealthy. He was an unacceptable match for his mother according to her family, but his knowledge and love of horses and horse racing won over Wes's grandfather.

Emma brought him the glass, her expression slightly guarded. When he took the glass from her, his fingers brushed hers, reminding him of their time together in his office that morning. He could claim that the touch was innocent, that it was an accident, but he would be lying to himself if he said he hadn't wanted to feel the softness and warmth of her fingers once more.

She pulled her hand away as soon as she possibly could. He wasn't the only one affected by their contact. It was satisfying for him to know that. Whatever kind of madness this was, they were experiencing it together.

"Do you want to talk about the house right now?" she asked.

"No," he said. "I don't want to interrupt your bread baking."

"You're right. Besides, how could you take me seriously? I must look a fright."

She had no idea how she looked to him. It was hard for him to take his eyes away from her.

He watched the women work in the kitchen for nearly an hour. If someone had told him that this was how he would spend his evening, he would have thought them insane. But he was enjoying himself. He liked listening to their chatter, their laughter. He liked to see the easiness between the three women. They were truly friends, in a way that women of his class weren't often allowed to be.

His class.

He didn't even know what that meant. His family was less than thrilled when they learned that he was choosing a career in medicine rather than one in business. Being a doctor was a respectable profession, but there wasn't much money in it. The sole goal for most of the men in his family was to increase their wealth.

Saving the world is the work of women, his grandfather once told him. Wes resented that. He resented a lot of things his family believed.

"Are you sure you're okay, Doctor?" Emma asked him. He didn't know when he had stopped thinking of her as Miss Cooke and started thinking of her as Emma, but he couldn't help himself.

"Call me Wes," he responded. "And yes, I am fine."

He had been coming home to quiet for so long—deep, oppressive quiet that was almost loud in a way. It was so different to sit here in the company of these women. He wasn't even listening to what they were saying, but their voices were comforting. The smell of the food cooking was soothing. He hadn't realized how out of sorts he had been feeling until now. There was no emptiness here.

"This food looks delicious, Caroline," Miss Dutton said. "I don't think I've ever been so excited to eat."

"You'll have my head swelling," Caroline said with a laugh.

"Are you sure you won't join us?" Emma asked her. "It seems unfair for you to do all the cooking and not get to enjoy it."

Caroline looked embarrassed. "You know it wouldn't be proper for me to eat with you."

"Proper?" Emma said. "There's nothing improper about sharing a meal with a new friend."

"I work for you, dear. Besides, I didn't do all the cooking. You helped. I also have my own children at home to feed. They wouldn't like it if I didn't eat with them."

"Of course. I feel terrible keeping you from your children."

"You aren't. It's my job." Caroline looked at Wes in disbelief. "Doctor, you have to explain to them how this works."

"It will take some getting used to," he said. "Everything smells wonderful. Thank you, Caroline."

"No need to thank me." She blushed. "I'll be taking the food over to Mr. Mercer now. He likes potatoes, so he should eat tonight."

"Hopefully," he said.

Soon Caroline was off for the night, leaving him with Emma and Miss Dutton. By rights, it should have been an awkward meal, but it was far from it. Miss Dutton was full of conversation and stories. Emma was more reserved but not quiet.

They enjoyed their hearty meal of chicken, mashed potatoes, and roasted carrots, all accompanied by the crusty bread the women had made.

It was a pleasant evening. Far more pleasant than he had had in a long while. He found himself lingering over his meal, not ready for it to end. But after a while the plates emptied, their stomachs were filled, and their conversation slowed.

Wes stood up and cleared the plates from the table. "Dr. Black," Emma said with astonishment in her voice, "you don't have to do that." She rushed from her seat and stood beside him.

"Clear the plates? Why not? My hands aren't broken. I do it every night at my house. And before Caroline started to cook for me, I cooked for myself."

"But you're a Prescott."

"I am also a doctor who has seen things that shouldn't be discussed in the company of ladies. Clearing the dishes is no hardship."

"I suppose, but you are a guest. You should let me do that."

He stepped around her and went to the sink, where he began to wash the dishes. "Right now is the perfect time to sit on the porch," he told them. "I believe there are still rocking chairs there. They should not sit empty."

Emma walked out to the porch with Mary moments later.

"I can't believe it," Emma said. "He is washing the dishes. If his aunt knew what he was doing, she would probably haunt me from her grave."

"I'm sure he's washed far worse. He's done surgery. I can't imagine a little gravy will turn his stomach."

"He is the most confusing man." Emma sat down rather indelicately in the rocking chair. "It's almost infuriating how confusing he is."

"He seems like a nice man. He's led an interesting life."

"But why is he being so nice?"

"Some people are nice." Mary shrugged. "There doesn't have to be a reason for it."

But she had seen him be not nice. She had seen him go from cold to warm and back to cold at an alarming speed. "Maybe it is because you are here. He thinks I stole his aunt's house. He's just pretending to be nice to me."

"I don't think the doctor has it in him to pretend. What does he have to gain from that?"

She didn't know, but there was no reason for him to still be there. Yes, she had been baking bread when he came, but she was ready and willing to stop to discuss whatever plan he had to learn the truth of her inheritance. But it seemed he wasn't ready to discuss the matter. He had watched them. Particularly her. She felt his eyes on her. His gazed contained warmth in it, and she could feel it on her skin. It was almost too much, and every time she looked up at him, his eyes met hers. She couldn't read them. It was disconcerting.

She wasn't one for vanity, but she was keenly aware of how frightful she must have looked. Covered in flour. Hair escaping its pins.

It was no wonder he didn't believe his aunt would leave her home to someone like her. Why would she?

"I believe he thinks you are beautiful."

Emma felt embarrassed by the thought. "You're being silly."

"I'm not! He wasn't looking at me the way he was looking at you."

"He doesn't think you are the evil woman who stole his aunt's house."

"Two things can be true at once. He could think you are beautiful and think you are the evil woman who stole his aunt's house."

Emma laughed. "I am very grateful you are here. I would be a blubbering mess hiding under my bed if it wasn't for you."

"You don't give yourself enough credit. You are a tough one. Don't forget it."

"I know you wanted to write to your aunt this evening. Please don't let me keep you from it."

"Yes, thank you." Mary stood up and took a step toward the door before she paused. "Tomorrow I'll need to make some preparations for my trip to Boston. I leave in two days. Are you sure you won't come with me?"

"I'm sure. You can enjoy your time without worrying about me. Besides, if I leave town right now, the good doctor will surely think I am guilty of something."

Mary grinned at her. "I'm excited to sleep in such a beautiful room. My grandmother's entire farmhouse would fit into the dining room alone. I will fall asleep feeling like a queen." Mary opened the front door only to nearly run into Dr. Black—Wes, he'd told Emma to call him.

Wes... It must be short for Wesley. She didn't think it suited him. It sounded boyish to her. Dr. Black, with his often grim face, was far from boyish. But she had seen a smile on his face tonight. He was handsome without it, but it had transformed his entire countenance. She would like to see him smile again.

"Doctor," Mary said, "I have some letters to write this evening, so I will say good night to you now."

"Good night, Miss Dutton. I enjoyed dining with you."

"And I with you."

He stepped aside to let Mary into the house. He didn't say a word to Emma but eased himself into the chair beside her. The chairs were close together. Perhaps too close. If she extended her arm a few inches, she could touch him.

"What is this about you leaving town?"

"I am not leaving town, and you were eavesdropping. Did you hope to hear more of my nefarious plan?"

"I wasn't eavesdropping. I overheard you, and clearly not well enough, because I only heard that bit of it."

"Mary is going to visit her cousin in Boston. She has expressed concern over leaving me here alone for a week."

"You aren't alone."

"I am. All the other teachers have gone home or are traveling. Mary has only extended family who live far from here, and I have no family at all. We have become each other's family."

"You mean a great deal to each other."

"Yes. Don't you have anyone who means a great deal to you?"

"I had my aunt, but she is gone now." He kept his tone almost neutral, but Emma could hear the grief in his voice. She deeply understood the feeling.

"What about your mother?" she asked softly.

"My mother and I were never close. We send a few letters a year, but that is it."

"Was she close to your aunt?"

"No. My mother was the youngest sister. Aunt Virginia thought she was terribly spoiled. And she was, by her father and then by my own father. My mother is the type of woman who needs a man to pamper her. My aunt never understood that."

"Your aunt was never married, was she?"

"No." He smiled. "I'm not sure God created a man strong enough to be her husband. She couldn't tolerate a weak-willed man. She wanted someone who could equal her in strength. He never came, and she never settled. She lived most of her adult life alone, which is rare for a woman to do."

"I wonder if she was ever lonely." The words slipped out of her mouth. She wished she hadn't said them.

"Perhaps she was," Wes said. "She would never admit it though."

"It would have been weak for her to," Emma said. "At least in her eyes."

"Do you ever feel lonely?" he asked.

"Sometimes," she whispered, surprising herself. "Do you?"

"Sometimes," he responded. "My aunt admitted that she was in love once when she was very young. She never told me who the man was or what became of him. Only that her father didn't approve of the match and that she obeyed his wishes. I sometimes find myself wondering about that man. He had to have been special. I don't think she ever allowed herself to love anyone else."

"Your aunt was a radical in a way, wasn't she? Most women would have settled, just for comfort and appearances. Your aunt didn't seem to care what anyone else thought."

"Our extended family found it curious the causes she chose to champion. She was passionate about educating girls, and she was getting heavily involved in the suffrage movement before she fell ill."

"I am sad she is gone," Emma said truthfully.

"I am too." Wes looked at her for a long moment before he stood up. "I should be heading home now."

She was surprised by his abruptness. "But I thought you wanted to discuss a plan for learning the truth about my inheritance."

"I do," he said quietly. "But not tonight. Good night, Miss Cooke."

"Emma," she replied.

"Good night, Emma."

"Good night, Wes."

He nodded at her and walked away. Emma was more confused than ever.

⁓ CHAPTER SIX ⁓

Finally, be ye all of one mind, having compassion one of another,
love as brethren, be pitiful, be courteous.
—*1 Peter 3:8*

Wes gently turned the little girl's ankle from side to side. Abigail, Abby for short, let out a little yelp as he did.

Her father had rushed her to his office a few minutes ago, his face full of panic. Wes was just about to leave for his house calls when they came in.

"I'm sorry, Abby," he said. "I'm nearly done." He felt to see if there were signs of any broken bones in her foot. "How did you say this happened, Mr. Chambers?"

"She was running after the chickens with her brothers, and her ankle just bent right beneath her. I've never seen a foot do that before. I was sure it was broken."

"It's quite swollen." He heard the front door open, but he didn't look up to see who it was. "I'm sure it hurts like the dickens, Abby."

"Like the dickens," the little girl agreed. She couldn't have been more than four. She had very round and very wet, red cheeks. Her fine blond hair was plastered to her face from the tears. Even in this state she was as cute as she could be.

"We have to be careful when chasing chickens."

"Toby said I couldn't catch one. I wanted to show him I could."

"I'm sure you could have if it wasn't for this ankle. But, unfortunately, there will be no more chasing chickens for you for a very long time."

"A very long time?" she repeated with wide eyes.

"A very, very long time," he said. "You see how your ankle is turning purple?"

Abby nodded and wiped her nose on her sleeve.

"It's twice its normal size. We need for all the swelling to go away. In order for that to happen, you mustn't walk on it." He turned to look at Abby's father. "Mr. Chambers, I am prescribing that you must carry Abby everywhere she needs to go. And her brother Toby must give her a piggyback ride or carry her on his shoulders. She cannot walk on this foot. It would be very bad if she does."

"Piggyback rides?" Wes could see a wobbly smile forming on Abby's face.

"Yes, but he must be very careful not to hurt your ankle. It needs to heal."

"How long, Doctor?" Mr. Chambers asked.

"At least a month. Maybe longer. I will wrap it today, and then I will visit her next week to check on it. Sprains can sometimes be worse than a break. It is very important that she stay off her foot. If it doesn't heal properly, she might have trouble walking later on."

"I understand, Doctor." Mr. Chambers nodded.

"Do you understand, Abby? You need to rest this foot. No walking or hopping on it. You mustn't give your mother a hard time about it either."

"I won't. I'll be a good girl."

"I know you will be." He stood to retrieve the wrapping for her foot, but he didn't have the chance to go far, because suddenly Emma was there, the bandage in her hand.

"Is this the right one, Doctor?" she asked.

He was truly surprised to see her there. She was tidier than she had been last night. Not a trace of flour in sight. "It is the right one. Thank you."

He quickly wrapped Abby's ankle and gave her father a few tablets to give her. "She'll likely be in pain for the first few days, so she won't try to walk on it, but I need her to stay off her foot even after the pain and swelling subsides."

"I understand. I'll make sure of it." He picked Abby up in his arms as if she were a baby. He supposed she was *his* baby. "Tell the doctor thank you, Abby."

"Thank you for fixing my ankle, Dr. Black. I promise I won't make you cross."

"I'm sure you won't. I will come check on you in a few days."

The father and daughter left, and soon Wes found himself alone with Emma.

"You were very kind to her," Emma said. "I must admit to being surprised. You've seemed quite grim to me."

"Have I? You've known me a total of three days. Have I been grim every moment of it?"

"No. I may have only officially known you for three days, but I know you are a very serious man."

"You are a serious woman. You chose mathematics as your field. I can't think of a less joyful subject."

"I didn't choose mathematics. It was chosen for me."

"For you?"

"My father learned that I could multiply large numbers in my head when I was about the age of your little patient that just left. So he had me tutored and tutored and tutored. I continued to excel in the subject, but I'd much rather paint or play piano or sing. But mathematics is more useful, according to my father."

"Your father, the music master, thought math was more valuable than the arts."

"Artists often starve, he said. He thought I could take my skill with numbers and turn it into a respectable career. He always taught me that I needed to be able to take care of myself. That I couldn't rely on a husband. He made me promise before he died that I would complete my education."

"There was something that drove him to tell you that. Most men want their daughters to be taken care of by a husband."

"He never spoke much about his childhood, but I do believe his father was unable to take care of his family."

"Which is too often the case. I have been witness to more than a few accidents at the powder mill. One day the husband is there to take care of the family, the next a widow is left behind. It is never an easy life."

"No. I didn't mean to go off on a tangent, only to tell you that I was impressed with the way you handled the little girl. You spoke to her in a way she could understand. She wasn't afraid of you at all."

"Why should she be afraid of me? I'm her doctor."

"You're a large man. You loom over people. Your presence takes up the room. That could be intimidating to a little girl. It most certainly can be to an adult woman."

"It is not my aim to intimidate anyone. I am simply the way God made me."

She nodded. "Do you want children of your own?"

"Yes, I would like many of them." He smiled. "I say that as an only child who always wanted a sibling. I might not enjoy a house full of noisy children in reality."

"I like the noise. At school the girls are always laughing and chattering. I couldn't wait for the term to end so I could have a quiet moment, but I don't like it as much as I thought I would. I miss the girls. I miss their noise."

If she was a con artist, she was the sweetest one ever invented. "Absence makes the heart grow fonder. They will return."

"There you go, getting me offtrack again. I didn't come for a social visit. I came to ask you a question, and then I will be on my way."

He didn't want her to be on her way. He wasn't ready for her to go. He had told himself he wouldn't see her today, even though this investigation was his idea and the curiosity of her inheritance was eating at him. The pleasantness of last evening made him not want to spoil the feeling he had. "I will try my best to answer."

She pulled a key from her pocket. "Do you have any idea what this key goes to?"

It was the ornate brass key he had seen the other day. It stood out from the rest. It seemed special. "No, I have no idea. Did you ask John?"

"Yes, and Caroline. Neither of them knows where it belongs. It doesn't fit any of the outside doors."

"I'm sorry. I can't help you with that."

"There is nothing personal of your aunt left behind. I slept in her bedroom. But there wasn't a single trace of her. Not a hairbrush, not a pin, not an ounce of clothing. It's as if she was never in that bedroom at all."

"Have you looked through the rest of the house?"

"I haven't," she said. "It feels like snooping. There aren't family portraits on the walls either. I was there at Christmas but didn't pay attention. Was it much different before?"

"The family portraits are all at the mansion in Newport, which my grandfather's youngest brother now owns. I haven't been in all the bedrooms. I couldn't tell you what was in them."

"Your family isn't from this area, so why did your aunt decide to build her home here? Newport to Hazardville is no small change. Did it not seem odd to you when she chose it?"

"My aunt had a home in Hartford where she spent the majority of her time. She was good friends with the Beecher family. Reverend Lyman Beecher, the famous abolitionist, was the patriarch. I believe that Aunt Virginia attended Litchfield Female Academy with his daughters and decided that she preferred life in Connecticut to life in Newport. As for Hazardville, I think she was part owner in the powder mill. She would never discuss business. She thought it was unbecoming. That is her only connection to this place that I can think of."

"Interesting." Emma nodded. He could see her thinking, or maybe calculating was the correct term for the mathematician. "She owned her home in Hartford?"

"Yes."

"Do you know who inherited it?"

Wes paused. He hadn't thought about it. "I don't know."

"Did you read her will?"

"No, I—"

"You don't know how she distributed the rest of her estate? I assume that a woman with her means had quite a substantial one. You only know for sure that I was given this house and you were given a stable of horses. What about the Hartford house? What about her home in the Caribbean? Maybe she gave those away to strangers too. Have you considered that?"

"I—"

"Have you contacted your mother?"

"She is in France. She cannot be easily reached."

"You could have sent a telegraph. You could have found a way to communicate with her. Your aunt was her sister. I'm sure a lawyer has already delivered the news of her death."

"I did not expect you to be so interested in this matter."

"This matter? She didn't leave me a brooch. She changed my life with this gift. You didn't think I would be interested in learning the truth about it? You just chose to believe that I somehow took advantage of her without knowing any of the facts."

"So I was just supposed to believe you? How do I know you are who you say you are? This could all be an elaborate ruse."

"You should at least have come armed with facts before you made an accusation like that. I may not be as respected as you in this community, but I am a decent woman who values her reputation. I will not have it smeared by you. I will prove to you that I am innocent."

"You do that. You do all the investigating you want, but I will not believe you until I have verified the information on my own."

"There's no point in continuing this conversation. You do whatever you need to do."

She turned to leave. But he wasn't ready for that to be the end of it. "What's 4,283 times 320?"

"That's an easy one," she said. "The answer is 1,370,560. If you're going to test me, at least make it challenging."

"You just made that number up," he called after her.

She didn't respond. Her answer had sounded so confident. He rushed over to his desk and scribbled the problem on a piece of paper. It annoyed him that she was right. Not just about the multiplication problem but about the entire situation.

He needed to forget about his silly attraction to her and get serious about solving the mystery that was his aunt.

Pompous man.

Emma marched out of the doctor's office, the need to be rid of his presence overwhelming her. She wanted to breathe air that wasn't infected with his smugness.

He was the most annoying man she had ever met.

He was the one who hadn't bothered to learn anything and then had the unmitigated gall to try to test her. He was still probably at his desk trying to figure out the answer to the question he gave her. He could have ended this all yesterday if he had just agreed to take the house when she offered.

He claimed he didn't want it, and she believed him. He didn't seem like a man who cared for material possessions. He seemed like the type who loved to extend torture for indefinite periods of time. She pushed to the back of her mind the pictures she had of him and his very young patient. None of that mattered.

How could he not have checked to see who else his aunt left her properties to? They had to go to someone. A house in Hartford. One in the Caribbean. Part ownership in the powder mill. Who knew how many other properties she had in her holdings? The lawyer hadn't given her the entire will, just the documents pertaining to her situation. Was she entitled to see the entire thing? It could give her some clues as to why she received the house. Maybe there was some connection to the other recipients of Miss Prescott's gifts.

Emma had felt like a criminal even doing the very minor searching of the bedroom she slept in last night. The house didn't yet feel like it belonged to her. She had felt as if she didn't have the right to go snooping around. But all that was over. She couldn't be so circumspect anymore. There were too many questions to be answered.

There had to be a trace of Miss Prescott somewhere in that house. There must be some kind of clue as to why she chose a virtual stranger to be her heir. There were so many thoughts rattling around in her head she didn't know how to begin to sort them out.

She only knew that she was angry and her face felt hot and she missed her father right now. She wished she could talk to him. She wished she could rest her head on his shoulder like she did when she was a little girl and let his deep, warm voice calm her.

But he had been gone for six years now. And it was times like this when she felt most alone. She must have been walking for some time now. She had no direction in mind, but she didn't head back to the house or to the inn, or even to the banks of the Scantic, which sometimes soothed her. She found herself heading to the church. It had been built a few years before she was born. Big, beautiful red-brick with white spires, it was in the Gothic Revival style. Emma found the building welcoming and soothing.

She walked up the steps and opened the door. There was no one there. It was blissfully quiet. She took her familiar seat in the last pew and closed her eyes. The thoughts started to drift from her head. There was no one to judge her here. No one to look down on her. No one to accuse her. There was peace in this building. She carried God with her everywhere she went, but she felt more of Him in this place, and she wished she could bottle this peacefulness and sip from it whenever she felt depleted.

She wasn't sure how long she sat there. But she felt like she was no longer alone. She opened her eyes to see Pastor Barker standing a few feet in front of her.

"Miss Cooke. I hope I didn't startle you. I just wanted to see if you were okay."

"I am." She shook her head. "No. That is not true. Did you know Miss Prescott?"

"Not well, unfortunately. She was always exceedingly polite, but she didn't attend services here regularly, and when she did, she did not interact with the community much."

"That is what I have come to learn about her. No one here knew her well, and now she is gone."

"I heard that she went home to the Lord, and I wondered if it was true."

"Yes." She nodded, surprised at the sadness she felt about it. She didn't know the woman, and yet she felt her loss. It almost made the weight of her gift even heavier. "She left me her house."

Pastor Miller's eyes widened. "The house on School Street?"

"Yes. A lawyer came and handed me the keys and the deed. I am having trouble processing it."

"I wasn't aware that you were close to her."

"I wasn't close to her. I only met her a few times. I cannot fathom why she would leave me her house."

"Have you spoken to Dr. Black? He is her nephew. He might have some insight."

"I have spoken to the doctor. He doesn't believe that his aunt would leave me her house of her own volition. He thinks I conned his aunt into giving it to me."

"Of course you didn't. Would you like me to speak to him on your behalf?"

"No. Please don't. There is nothing anyone can say to change his mind. He will require proof."

"What can the proof be?"

"That is a good question." She thought for a moment. "Do you have any idea why Miss Prescott chose to build a house here? She had a house in Hartford, only twenty miles away. Dr. Black said she invested in the powder mill, but most investors do not move to the town their investments are in."

"Maybe it was impulsive. Maybe she found the town charming and decided to make a home here."

"I have a feeling nothing Miss Prescott did was impulsive."

"You might be right about that."

"Are wills a matter of public record?"

"I believe so, but I cannot be sure. I do know someone who might be able to help you. My brother-in-law is visiting from Hartford, and he is a lawyer. He might be able to offer some insight."

"Oh, that would be wonderful. Would you be willing to set up a meeting?"

"Yes. I can bring him to the inn later this afternoon."

"Please bring him to the house on School Street. That is where I will be staying until we sort this all out."

CHAPTER SEVEN

If we confess our sins, he is faithful and just to forgive us our sins,
and to cleanse us from all unrighteousness.
—1 John 1:9

"Dr. Black?" Tim called from the doorway of Wes's office. "I'm heading home for the evening. Is there anything you need before I go?"

"No. Thank you, Tim. Have a good evening."

"I hope you don't think I'm being intrusive, but you seem out of sorts today. I renew my suggestion for you to take some time off. I can handle things alone for the next few days."

"I am out of sorts," he admitted. "But I don't think taking extra time off will set me right. In fact, I think it might do the opposite."

It would give him more time to think, and that was the last thing he wanted. He wished his mind could be peacefully blank, but it was far from that today. So many thoughts inundated him, and those thoughts were accompanied by guilt. And grief. He hadn't admitted that to himself before, but it was there, and it was heavy.

"I didn't come here to lecture you. I'm simply here to remind you that if you need me to take on more responsibilities for a while, I am more than willing to."

"Thank you, Tim. I know that. That's why I hired you. You are a good doctor. I don't say it often, but know that you are."

"Thank you."

Wes was prepared to leave it at that, but then he said, "I always thought I was close to my aunt, but now that she is gone, I am finding that I didn't know her very well. That I may have known her just as everyone else knew her, on the surface."

Emma was right. His aunt had other homes, other holdings in other places around the world. He didn't know where any of her other properties went. He didn't know if his mother was left anything. His cousins. His uncle, who had a family. A well-known, wealthy family. They were not close though.

He knew so little outside of the small world he had made for himself. He considered himself an educated man, but he was ignorant about what really counted.

"Sometimes our relatives keep things from us because they are trying to protect us," Tim said. "Or maybe because they think it's simply not our business. But many times it is hard for people to share, so they do not say anything at all."

Wes understood Tim's point all too well. "Do you remember Miss Cooke from the other day?"

"The teacher? Yes." He nodded. "I found her to be very pleasant."

"She inherited my aunt's house. She claims not to know my aunt, and I find it very suspicious that Aunt Virginia would give her a house that took her nearly two years to build."

"Surely there must be a will."

"There is, but neither of us were given the entire will. Only the papers that pertained to us. I have accused her of something that she might very well be innocent of."

"It is natural to be suspicious under these circumstances. Especially if your aunt wasn't in the practice of such generous gift giving."

"But that's the issue. Maybe she was in the practice of generous gift giving. Maybe I didn't know her nearly as well as I thought I did. As I sit here with these thoughts churning in my head, it's becoming clearer and clearer that I did not. I don't know why she moved to Hazardville. I also never bothered to ask her. She encouraged me to open my practice here because there was a definite need, but I never questioned why she moved here in the first place."

"It's a lovely town. Maybe she just enjoyed her time here."

"She had a home in Hartford and one in the Caribbean. She has an apartment in our family home in Newport, and yet she built a large house here. She went back and forth to Hartford so often, I wager she didn't spend more than thirty nights in this house before she left for the Caribbean."

"And Miss Cooke can offer you no insight?"

"None. She has come to me for answers, which has only led to more questions."

"I'm fairly new to town, but I haven't heard anything bad about Miss Cooke."

"No one has heard a bad thing about her or has a bad thing to say. I asked a few of the chattier patients when I was on my calls today. When school is in session, she spends most of her time with her students, and then she goes home to the inn. Sometimes she ventures to the shops to buy herself a few sweets or some fabric. The only other place she goes is to church. She has led a very quiet, very unexceptional life since she has been here."

"And before she was here?"

"I have someone looking into that. It might take a while to hear back."

"I understand that the school is closed for the summer, but there are still members of the board in town. I believe Mrs. Ellison, the magistrate's wife, is on the board. You might inquire with her as to why they hired her."

"That is a brilliant idea. I will go ask her, though it is probably too late to call on her tonight."

"She is a regular attendee at the church. I know from her husband that she likes to get there early. You might be able to catch her before service starts."

"But I might run into Miss Cooke there," he said before he could stop himself.

"Is that a problem?"

"I've been doing a lot of thinking about our last meeting and am embarrassed by my behavior."

"Well then, Dr. Black, the right thing to do would be to apologize."

He knew Tim was right. He knew he should apologize. He was allowed to be suspicious of her without being rude. But Emma was no regular woman, and when he was anywhere near her, he didn't have regular feelings. He felt more. Often too much and, after feeling numb for some time, it was overwhelming for him. He forgot himself.

"You're right, Tim. It's appears as though I'll be heading to church tomorrow for more than one reason."

The next morning, Wes left his house and walked to the church. It was on the other side of Hazardville, but he chose to walk there instead of taking his horse and gig. He could use the exercise. It was peaceful outside at this time of the morning. The only things he could hear around him were the chirping of birds and the rustling of wind through the leaves. He wasn't sure if he was ever going to learn the answer to why his aunt chose to move here or why she convinced him to open his practice here. But he was glad that he had listened to her.

He had gone to medical school in Boston and worked his first job there, but he had been unhappy. He never said it to his aunt or even admitted it to himself. There were so many people and so little time he could spend with each patient. There was no establishing relationships. No seeing families grow, no sense of community. He had worked at Boston City Hospital, and while he liked the idea of working in a place that serviced the poor, he didn't like the emptiness of never knowing what happened to them after they left his care.

In Hazardville, it was the opposite. He knew the people of this town and was a part of their lives even if it was just in a small way. He'd found community here. It was something he didn't feel like he had in Newport growing up. There was too much wealth. Too much competition. He didn't feel comfortable in that world and never found a way to fit in.

He arrived at the church well before service started. The street was nearly empty. He wasn't sure if he should go inside and wait for Mrs. Ellison or stand outside until she arrived, but soon the choice was made for him. He heard the clomping footsteps of a horse and turned to see a buggy with a well-dressed woman in it pull up in front of the church.

Mrs. Ellison stepped down and said a brief word to the driver before he drove the buggy around to the back of the church.

"Dr. Black." She greeted him with a smile. "How lovely to see you here today. You are early for service. I like to have tea with Mrs. Barker before it starts. Would you care to join us?"

"No, thank you, ma'am. I was hoping to see you today though."

"Oh?" Her delicate brows raised. "How can I help you? This isn't about George, is it? He's the type of man to be sick and not tell me."

"Your husband is in perfect health."

She looked relieved. "How can I help you then?"

"I was told you are on the board for the Dixon Academy for Girls."

"I am."

"I was hoping to learn how you acquire teachers."

"The process can be intensive. We hire only female teachers. They must be educated and have very strong morals and values. Most of our current teachers applied, but some of them have come to us by recommendation."

"Did Miss Cooke apply to the school?"

"No, Miss Prescott recommended her. I don't know how she learned of her, but Miss Cooke was working at another school, and we approached her. It was our luck that she decided to join us. She is a brilliant mathematics teacher. I suspect if she were a man, she would be teaching at the university level."

His aunt had found her? "You check their backgrounds before you hire them?"

"Of course. Miss Cooke's former employer was quite upset she was leaving. He hired her after her graduation from Wesleyan University. His brother was her professor."

So, she was a real person. Her story could be proven. But none of that explained how his aunt knew her.

"Oh dear. Miss Prescott was your aunt, wasn't she? I often think of you just as Dr. Black. Not as her nephew. I am so sorry for your loss."

"Thank you, Mrs. Ellison. Did you know my aunt well?"

"I wish I could say I did. I sat with her on the board and attended a few social functions with her. She was quite an impressive woman, but I could not say we were friends."

It was the same story everyone in this town had. Who were his aunt's friends? Who really knew her? Who had insight into who she was?

Again, he had come for answers and only ended up with more questions.

"Thank you for your time, Mrs. Ellison. I didn't intend to keep you from your tea."

"I was pleased to speak with you today. We are truly sorry for your loss. Please let us know if we can do anything."

"Continue to be on the academy's board. It meant a great deal to my aunt."

She nodded. "I will. It means a great deal to me as well."

He watched her enter the church as more people were starting to arrive. He didn't often attend church. Everyone was so friendly, but he didn't know how to return the friendliness without feeling awkward.

He went inside before anyone could recognize him. He had gotten one of the items on his list accomplished. Now it was time to face the other.

Emma was a few minutes early for the service. She usually was. She liked to get there before the crowd and take her seat in the back pew.

But today, instead of finding her pew empty, she saw it was occupied by a now-too-familiar person.

"You're in my seat," she said.

Wes glared at her. "There is an entire pew here. I believe they were intended to fit more than one person. Besides, I don't see your name on it."

"Fine. I will find somewhere else to sit."

How dare he! She rarely saw him here. Maybe three times in the year she had been attending. He was always with his aunt, and he always sat in the front, which was reserved for the town's important members. What was he doing here in the back? In her space. She came to church to find peace. There was no way she could find solace with him sitting here.

"Emma." He grabbed her hand just as she started to turn away. "Please."

She looked down at him. There was something in his expression that made her pause. He seemed tired. Not just sleepy but almost weary.

She understood the feeling. She was feeling the same way.

She looked down at her hand, which was still enclosed in his. He let go quickly. They were in public. In church. Most of the congregation might not take note of her, but they definitely would notice him. He was their doctor. And while his touch might be innocent, it might not be seen as proper.

"I beg your pardon," he said gruffly. "Please, sit."

She did as he asked, feeling the warmth of his body as she sat next to him. He made her feel uncomfortable and yet drawn to him at the same time. No one else had ever made her feel this way.

She didn't want to think about what that could mean. "Why are you here?"

"I need to apologize to you. I seem to behave poorly whenever I am around you. You haven't done anything to deserve it."

"I—" She didn't know what to say. "Thank you. I appreciate that."

"Part of me wishes I'd never met you. You make me question everything. You make me realize I don't know as much about my aunt as I thought I did. I have been unable to turn my thoughts off since I met you. Everything centers around you."

His words snatched the air from her lungs. She couldn't ask him what he meant by that, because the pews around them had filled and the minister walked out, ready to start the service.

They both fell quiet. It was hard to concentrate on the Scripture reading. She was no closer to solving the mystery of the gifted house than when she started. She had spoken to Pastor Miller's brother-in-law the other day. He requested a full copy of Miss Prescott's will directly from her attorney on Emma's behalf. She wasn't sure how long the request would take to get to New York City or how long it would be until the will arrived. So she would just have to wait. But even if she was able to read the entire will, it might not contain the answers she was seeking. It could just pose more questions. It seemed no one really knew Miss Prescott well. Not in Hazardville at least. From what Pastor Miller's brother-in-law told her, even in Hartford where she spent most of her time, her friends were more like close acquaintances. They worked together on social causes. They dined together. Attended the same events. But they didn't know anything about her personal life. There wasn't even gossip surrounding her.

The woman was a mystery.

The organ started to play a hymn.

Wes started to sing along with the rest of the congregation. She was so surprised, she turned to look at him. He had a lovely deep voice. He looked back at her. Right into her eyes, which made her stomach get that fluttery feeling that she could never name.

He raised both his brows at her, which for some reason made her smile. She started to sing with him. This was her favorite part of the service. And finally, after feeling restless for the past day or so, the music took over, and she felt soothed.

The service lasted an hour, and by the end of it, her spirits were lifted. Going to church always helped her mood, but today there was something else. With Wes sitting beside her, she hadn't felt alone. It was comforting to hear his clear baritone voice, feel his warm presence beside her.

She had been angry with him since she left his office, but holding on to that anger was tiring. It drained her. They had the same goal but for opposite reasons. They were enemies of sorts, and she didn't want that. But she also didn't see how it was possible that they could be friends.

They both stood and left the pew. A man called Wes's name, and he went off to greet him. It made sense for them to go their separate ways now. He'd apologized. She'd accepted. That was that.

Emma made her way to the door. She waved to some of the parishioners she was familiar with but didn't stop to talk like most people usually did after the service.

Mrs. Ellison, the magistrate's wife and a member of the academy's board, stopped her just as she descended the steps of the church.

"Miss Cooke!" She gave her a big smile.

"Hello, Mrs. Ellison. It was a lovely service today, was it not?"

"Yes, it was. I felt that the congregation sounded especially joyful when singing this morning."

"I agree. It is always my favorite part of the service."

"I noticed that Dr. Black sat next to you. He rarely comes to church."

Of course it hadn't gone unnoticed. Wes might be a quiet man, but everyone was aware of who he was and what he did. "I was surprised to see him as well."

"He was asking me about you."

She nodded, feeling disappointed, though she wasn't sure why. It was well within his rights to inquire about her, and Mrs. Millwright was the best person in town to ask. She knew a little bit about everyone in the community. "His aunt left me a gift in her will. I'm sure he was just trying to determine why she did."

"Maybe." She smiled, looped her arm through Emma's, and led her away from others who were in earshot. "I believe Dr. Black is interested in courting you."

"No!" She was shocked. "He didn't say that, did he?"

"Oh my dear, men like Dr. Black don't simply admit these things. He is more subtle. You got him to come to church. Voluntarily. That was how I knew my George was serious about me. He found his way back to the Lord."

"I'm sure it was just a coincidence."

"Do you not want Dr. Black to court you?" Her eyes widened. "Has he done something offensive?"

"He is a gentleman. I just don't think he is interested in me like that."

"Why not? You are a lovely woman. Educated, respectable, kind. You aren't a schoolgirl, just out of the schoolroom. You are a good match for Dr. Black. He needs a wife, and you need a husband."

"I think we are both fine individually and are not in need of each other."

"I've embarrassed you, haven't I? I didn't mean to. I've only come to offer my help."

"Help?"

"You do not have any relatives to assist in this courtship, so I am offering myself. I could arrange a dinner or maybe a picnic. It will give you two an opportunity to get to know each other."

"I appreciate you trying to assist me, but please, do not go out of your way. I do not think the doctor is interested in courting me. He is very protective of his aunt, and I believe he wants to know how I was involved with her."

"All right, Miss Cooke," she said with a smile. "I overwhelmed you. Think about what I have said and know my offer still stands if ever you want to take it. I believe the members of our board would be delighted if one of our teachers ended up married to the most eligible man in town."

Emma's cheeks felt hot, but she managed to smile and nod her head. "Thank you, Mrs. Ellison. I appreciate that."

She quickly walked away from the woman, praying no one had heard their conversation. Most of the crowd had cleared out, and Emma was thankful she didn't have to stop to speak to anyone else. She started to make her way toward the house, her house, as it was for now. She was slowly starting to fall in love with the place. It was a far cry from the room she rented at the inn. She had lived in small rooms since she was eighteen years old. There was never much space for more than a bed and a chair. But now she was living in a house with more rooms than she knew what to do with. She wished her father could see it.

"Slow down," she heard. "You look as if you're about to break into a sprint."

She turned to see Wes coming up beside her. She was surprised to see him again. "I thought you would be halfway home by now."

"It's a beautiful day and my day off. There's no reason for me to go home so soon."

"Your presence in church today caused quite a stir. At least with Mrs. Ellison."

"I asked her about you. You were right. I shouldn't have accused you without knowing all the facts."

"And what did you learn?"

"That my aunt was the one who recommended you for the job here."

"She did?" That was news to her.

"Apparently. That answered one question but led to another and another."

"Yes." She nodded. "Why did she recommend me? How did she find me?"

"You understand."

"This mystery grows more frustrating by the day." She looked up at him. "Mrs. Ellison thinks you are interested in courting me and has offered her services as a matchmaker."

"That's ridiculous!"

She felt slightly stung by his response. "That's what I told her."

"Why would I need her to play matchmaker?" He frowned. "You are not a child. I am thirty years old. We do not need interference from the town's busybody."

It was her turn to frown. "I am very confused by this conversation. Are you courting me?"

"Do you want to be courted by me?" he countered.

"Answer my question first."

"I choose not to. Will you accompany me somewhere?"

As exasperating as he was, she did not want to go back to her big empty house alone. Mary had left for her trip to Boston. It was Caroline and John's day off. "Yes."

He led her off the street and onto a well-worn path in the woods. "You aren't going to ask me where we are going?"

"Do I need to be worried?"

"When you are with me, you never need to worry," he said so confidently it made her laugh.

"Now I am less reassured than before."

He grinned at her. There was a boyish quality trapped beneath the serious doctor. She wondered if anyone else got to see this side of him. If anyone ever got to see the softer side of him.

"Why did your aunt leave town?" The smile dropped from his face, and immediately she regretted her question. "I'm sorry. You don't have to answer that."

"I will answer it. She had cancer. It was quite progressed by the time I learned of it. I suspect she knew she was sick well before she got a diagnosis. My aunt had her pride. I believe she didn't want anyone to see her in a weakened state. Especially me. I think she didn't want me to remember her that way."

"But you would have remembered the whole woman, not just who she was at the end."

He stopped walking. "I never questioned her when she told me that she was going to spend her final days alone at her island home. Aunt Virginia always did what she wanted, and no one could change her mind about it." His voice caught, and he paused for a moment. "I regret not trying to change her mind." He tried to compose himself, but Emma could see that the emotion was still there. "I regret not being with her as she went to God. I can't help but think that she died without ever hearing me say that I loved her."

Emma took Wes's hand. He was deeply feeling the loss of someone he loved. She felt the loss with him. She had experienced it as well.

"I'm sure she knew you loved her," she said after a while. She didn't know how long they stood there, holding hands, but she didn't want to let him go. She felt safe. She felt content. She had led a relatively quiet life these past few years, but she hadn't felt safe with anyone since her father died.

Why did she feel safe with him?

They were on opposite sides. They didn't trust each other. And yet, the pull between them was undeniably strong.

He raised her hand and kissed the back of it. "You do something to me that I can't explain. I do not like it." He started walking down the trail again, still holding her hand. "I wrote to my mother because of you," he said. "I told her that I would like to see her again."

"Are you going to go to France?"

"If I must, but I was hoping she would come here. I would like to have some sort of service for my aunt in Newport. I would like you to be there as well."

"Me?" she asked, surprised. "Your family will be there."

"Which is precisely why I want you to be there."

It was such a confusing invitation. One that made her mind rush with questions she was too scared to think about in the moment.

"But you don't even trust me."

"Who feels like being rational right now?"

"I don't understand you," she said, shaking her head with a smile.

"I don't understand myself."

He continued to lead her through the woods for a while until they came to a small clearing. There was a small cluster of tiny homes, some of them no bigger than a room. He let go of her hand.

"It is not as isolated here as it seems. There is a road on the other side of the last house that leads into town. All the people who live here are connected to the powder mill. These houses were built by the first people the mill brought over from England. Mr. Mercer was one of them. He was just a boy then, and now he is my oldest patient."

"Mr. Mercer? I heard Caroline say she had to make extra soup to take to a Mr. Mercer. You pay her to cook for him, don't you?"

"I am his doctor. I prescribed him two hearty meals a day. I would do the same for any patient." He walked to the house on the end of the row. It was in worse shape than the other houses, which looked lived in and cared for. This one looked neglected. Wes knocked on the door twice before they heard a grunt that let him know it was okay for them to come in.

She spotted Mr. Mercer sitting at a small table in the corner. He sat up a little straighter. Something flashed in his eyes just for a moment that looked suspiciously like happiness, but it soon was replaced by a neutral expression. Without him saying a word she could tell Mr. Mercer was a proud man.

"Doctor." He nodded.

"Mr. Mercer." Wes nodded back. "How are you feeling today, sir?"

"Same as yesterday and the day before that and the day before that." The man's thick accent was British, but not the posh accents she'd heard from some of her father's colleagues when she was growing up.

"Of course. Nothing to report, as usual."

"You brought a woman with you," he said, looking at Emma with some curiosity.

"Yes. My friend, Miss Emma Cooke. She is a teacher at the girls' school in town."

"That school is still open?"

"Yes, sir. It is."

"Don't see the need for it. If girls need to go to school, they can go to the one in town with the boys."

"There are hundreds of schools just for boys. Why shouldn't there be a few for girls?" Emma questioned, unable to not push back.

"I come from England. Home of Eton. That school shouldn't exist either. Just another place to separate the rich from the working man. A fancy school doesn't make one smarter. My Tillie was as smart as they came, and she never set foot in a school in her life."

"We don't only take rich students. We take all types of girls who want to learn. Giving them an education gives them options in life."

"Like what?"

"If my father hadn't educated me, I would have had to marry a man I didn't love just to be able to survive. I would have been miserable."

"Was there an actual man? Or are we talking about someone hypothetical?" Wes asked her.

"He was a colleague of my father. I was seventeen, he was forty. He told my father he would marry me so I would no longer be his burden. Shortly thereafter my father procured enough funds to send me to Wesleyan University. I have been able to support myself since I graduated."

"I suppose you think women should be able to vote too?" Mr. Mercer asked her.

"I do."

Mr. Mercer looked at Wes. "She's a handful."

"That she is."

"I think she can keep up with you."

"She drives me to the end of my sanity."

Mr. Mercer nodded and smiled. "Come sit here with me, Miss Cooke. I have bread and cream and jam."

Chapter Eight

Charity suffereth long, and is kind; charity envieth not;
charity vaunteth not itself, is not puffed up.
—1 Corinthians 13:4

Wes quietly walked beside Emma later that afternoon as they returned to the house.

It had somehow become "the" house in his head. Not his aunt's house. Not Emma's house either. Just some structure that had brought this woman into his life when he was least expecting it.

"You've gotten quiet," she said.

They had spent the better part of the day at Mr. Mercer's house. He didn't know what had driven him to take Emma to meet the old man, but he wanted him to know her. He wanted to let Emma in on this tiny private piece of his life.

"I'm just thinking."

"About what people might say about us? We have been in each other's company for most of the day."

"I wasn't thinking about that. But let them talk." He looked at her for a long moment. She was very beautiful in the afternoon light. He found her beautiful in all light, but especially today. She wore a deep blue dress that wasn't the height of fashion but showed off her slender waist. Her chestnut-brown hair was piled high on her head and secured with pins. She looked tidy. But he wondered what she would look like with her hair loose around her shoulders. He wondered what she looked like when she first woke up in the morning and what she looked like before she went to bed at night. He wondered what she looked like in her most vulnerable of moments. He wanted to see her in a way that no one else could.

These were troubling thoughts.

Why couldn't he have met her at church or at a dinner party?

Why was this blasted house and all its mysteries the thing that brought them together?

"You were very good with Mr. Mercer. I think he's eaten more today than he has all week."

"That is encouraging. I will do my best to get him to eat tomorrow when I bring him his food."

"You don't have to do that. I know you told him you would, but he will understand if you don't."

"Why would I not bring him his food?" She frowned at him. "You think I go around breaking promises?"

"Of course not. It's just—"

"It's just nothing. I will do as I said. I am not teaching at the moment, and besides, the house is not giving me any clues as to why it was given to me. I can spare the time."

"You've found nothing, then?"

"No. It would help if I knew what I was looking for. But there is nothing. No papers. No letters. No photographs. I have looked in every room. It is pristine."

"My aunt rented a smaller house just a street over while hers was being built. That is where I visited her the most when she was here. It has since been sold. Most of her possessions were probably in the Hartford house."

"Do you think you should take a trip to Hartford?"

"I have thought about it but dismissed it. I likely wouldn't be able to gain access to the Hartford house, and even if I did, I'm not sure there would be anything there."

"You could go and ask questions. You are her nephew and a doctor. You are also a man. People will speak to you. I think you should go."

The emotion was clear in her voice. He wanted to pull her into his arms and soothe away her anxiety. "This is important to you."

"It is only important to me because I don't want to look at you and wonder if you trust me. I don't want this hanging over our heads. I want to know the answer."

"What if there is no answer? Everything we have learned has only invited more questions."

"We need to exhaust every possibility."

"And then what?"

"And then…" She shook her head. "I don't know."

They approached the house. He wanted to go inside, but he knew he couldn't. He had already been gifted with enough of her time today. But he wouldn't be able to rest without knowing when he was going to see her again.

That was very troubling.

"I believe tomorrow afternoon I will have an undeniable urge for some jam cake around one o'clock."

"Jam cake does sound delightful," she said. "There is only one place in town that sells jam cake. I might also have an undeniable urge for it as well."

They smiled at each other. He couldn't recall another person he could share a smile with. He couldn't recall another person that he wanted to share a smile with.

"Dr. Black." She extended her hand to him. "I had a lovely day. Thank you for being a part of it."

He took her hand, but instead of shaking it, he ran his thumb over the backs of her delicate fingers and then stepped forward and placed a kiss on her cheek. He hadn't meant to do it. He knew he shouldn't have done it, but he couldn't stop himself.

She blushed, her cheeks turning the most attractive shade of pink.

"Wes…"

"I know." He squeezed her fingers. "I'll see you soon," he said before he walked away. He might have just sealed his fate, but he was feeling pretty good about it.

Over the next week, Wes found a reason to see Emma nearly every day. Sometimes he would run into her at Mr. Mercer's house. Other times she would meet him at his office for coffee before his first patient came in for the day. His favorite time to see her was in the evening after dinner. He walked to the house as if being pulled there by an unseen force. He would sit with her on the porch for hours until the sun set, talking about everything. People were starting to notice how much time the doctor and the teacher were spending together. They weren't being very discreet. They sat together on the porch for the world to see, waving at neighbors as they took walks on warm summer evenings.

Wes was normally a private man. But he didn't want to hide right now. He didn't want his time spent with Emma to be a secret. They weren't doing anything wrong. They were two adults brought together by some odd circumstances who were enjoying their time together.

There was a brief knock on his office door, and Tim's head appeared in the doorway. "Hello, Tim. How were your calls today?"

"Mrs. Jones is about to give birth any day now. I suspect twins. I told the midwife to send for one of us if any issues arise. Both women assured me there wouldn't be a need."

"Mrs. Jones is on her seventh pregnancy, if I am correct. She and the midwife have much more experience with the birthing process than we ever will."

"I suppose you are right. How is Miss Cooke today? I heard from Mrs. Ingle that you two were strolling along Main Street together."

"Does the entire town tell you my whereabouts whenever they see me with Miss Cooke?"

"Not the entire town, just the women over thirty." He grinned. "I do believe they are happy for you, Dr. Black."

"Wes. We do not need to stand on formality. Remember?"

"Wes." He nodded. "Everyone likes Miss Cooke, and it is hard not to notice how much more relaxed you are when you are in her company."

He couldn't fully express in words what he was feeling. He had worked so hard to become a doctor. So much of his life had been focused on his career. Nothing else seemed important. He had numbed himself to all outside forces. Sacrificing friendships, family, and mostly himself. And for what? What was the point of it all?

He hadn't been happy. He couldn't remember a time when he was. But now? Could what he now felt be the stirrings of happiness?

"Emma is a kind woman. I often wonder if she is just tolerating my company."

"She strikes me as the type of woman who doesn't tolerate unpleasant things."

"I hope you are right," he said with a smile.

"I am about to leave for the evening, but I came to tell you that a messenger came while you were out. He left a letter for you. I placed it on your desk."

There was a letter there, on top of a pile of correspondence that he needed to attend to. "I hadn't noticed the addition. Thank you for telling me."

"You're welcome. Have a good night, Wes. And for what it's worth, I am glad that Miss Cooke has come into your life."

He left before Wes could respond. But he couldn't agree more. He picked up the letter that had just been delivered. It had come from Hartford and, at first, he didn't recognize the name. But then he did. It was from the private investigator he had hired to learn the truth about Emma.

He looked at the letter for a long moment before putting it back down. He didn't want to open it. He didn't care what it said. Instead, he got up and walked out of the office. He had already seen her once today. But once wasn't enough. He headed toward the house again.

He was going to have to settle the mystery about the house sometime, but it wasn't going to be tonight.

The next morning, Emma sat at the piano in the formal living room. It was a beautiful instrument, and she could tell that Miss Prescott had spared no expense when she purchased it. It was a Steinway. The quality was incomparable. But why had she purchased it? This wasn't something a hobbyist or casual player purchased. It was what the best players in the world played. Her father had once taken a job just because there would be a Steinway at the school. He would be over the moon if he knew she got to live in a house with one. Play it whenever she chose.

Her father hadn't cared much for material possessions, but she knew if there was one thing he would have liked to own, it would have been this. What an odd coincidence that it was in the house she had been gifted.

She pressed the keys, hearing the melody of a song she couldn't remember the name of. Her father used to play this song. It was slow, sweet, and sad. A love song. She was never brave enough to ask him who he played it for, but she remembered hearing it often in the last year of his life.

"Excuse me, Miss Cooke," Caroline softly called to her.

Emma stopped playing and turned around.

"I hate to interrupt you, but I wanted to tell you that I've never heard anyone play as beautifully as you do. I love to hear you play as I go about my cleaning."

"Oh, thank you," Emma said, feeling slightly embarrassed. "I don't play as well as my father. He used to make people weep."

"I'm sure you are being modest. I would love it if one of my children had an ounce of your talent."

"Are any of them interested in playing an instrument?"

"My little one loves music, but she's only four. Too soon to tell."

"I started playing when I was three. Four is a perfect age. If you bring her to the house, I could teach her."

"Oh, I couldn't."

"Why not? I am a teacher. I enjoy teaching. It wouldn't be a long lesson. Just a few minutes at first until she gets comfortable with it."

"She's a handful. She'll make you want to pull out your hair."

"Caroline, if I can manage a roomful of adolescent girls who strongly dislike math, I think I can handle a four-year-old who enjoys music for a few minutes."

"Okay, then. I'll tell Beth about it tonight. I think she'll be excited." She pulled a thick envelope out of her apron. "This is the reason I came in. A messenger brought this. He said it was from New York City. It seemed important. I wanted to give it to you right away."

"Thank you, Caroline." She took the envelope from her and saw that it was what she had been waiting for. The complete copy of Miss Prescott's will.

She stared at the envelope in her hand long after Caroline left. She could open it right then, but she didn't want to do this alone. Wes had a right to know the contents of his aunt's will too. She had seen him nearly every day since he surprised her in church. She'd seen him for a few minutes in between patients yesterday, but last night, just when she started to miss him, he appeared on the porch. They'd sat outside all evening, until the sun had fully set. He stayed longer than he should have, but she didn't want him to go, and he didn't seem like he wanted to leave either.

Not once this week had they talked about the house or the dozens of questions surrounding it. It hung over their heads. Unspoken. It was the thing that was standing in between them. It had been blissful to ignore it. But it was unavoidable. They would have to face it eventually.

She left the house. It was still early. She might be able to catch him between patients.

When she arrived at his office, he was just finishing up with a young man who required stitches.

"You'll need to keep the area dry for at least twenty-four hours," Wes said in his low soothing voice. "After that you will need to wash it and pat the area dry."

"I will, Doctor," the young man said with a nod.

"I know it is a lot to ask a man to not work for a day, but if you could use your arm less it would help with the healing."

"I have tomorrow off. I will not move it at all, no matter how much my mother yells." He grinned.

"Good man." Wes grinned back. "If the redness gets worse or you experience swelling, pain, or bleeding, come see me immediately. That is a sign of infection."

"Thank you, Dr. Black. It might take us some time to pay you, but—"

"A dozen eggs."

"What?" The confusion was clear on the young man's face.

"A dozen eggs is what I am charging, and maybe a pie if your mother has time."

"Thank you." The young man stood and offered his hand to Wes. "You're a good man."

He was a good man. His calmness soothed his patients. People were more important than money. He was a healer. She could see God in him, and that wasn't something she could say about everyone.

The young man left, giving her a nod of acknowledgment on his way out. Wes's eyes zeroed in on her, and he crossed the room, not stopping till he reached her and pulled her into his arms. He pressed a kiss to her forehead, and she closed her eyes and enjoyed the way his warm, smooth lips felt against her skin. The safety of him blanketed her, and she didn't want to ever lose this feeling.

"This could get us in trouble," she said softly.

"In trouble? It's just a hug. I am happy to see you."

"Are you?"

"I told myself I was imposing my company on you too much and today I would give you a break."

"Did I somehow imply that I wanted or needed a break from you? I would have been very cross and wondering if I had done something wrong if you did not come see me today."

"Well, you are here and don't have to be cross, and I don't have to be a miserable man. I'm going to have to think of a way that I will be able to see you every day, any time of the day, without worrying about propriety. I wonder what I am going to do?"

Her heart... She couldn't describe the feeling. She had been alone for so long. So starved for somebody to care for her, to care for in return. But there was this...thing...between them.

"I came for a reason," she said pulling out of his arms but wishing she didn't have to. "I requested a full copy of your aunt's will. It arrived this morning. I was hoping it could give us some answers."

He sighed, and there was a world of meaning contained in that sigh. They could no longer pretend as if this mystery didn't exist. "Let's go into my office and take a look at it."

Instead of going to his desk, he guided her to the settee in the corner and sat beside her. It was a long document. They leaned against each other as they read. Some of the information they already knew or suspected. Some of it was new to them. Miss Prescott's jewels went to Wes's mother. The other houses were to be sold, and the proceeds were to fund scholarships for women and girls around the country. The shares in the powder mill went to her eldest brother. There were other, smaller, items—paintings, classic books, mementos from Miss Prescott's travels that went to various friends who understood the sentimental meaning of those gifts. Monetary gifts were left to girls' schools and to various women's organizations. The house here and the biggest part of her estate went to Emma. No explanation. Nothing was clearer than it was before.

"Well, it seems we are exactly where we started," Wes said after a long moment.

"I can't help but feel disappointed," Emma admitted. "I was hoping this could be the answer to all our questions and that we could put it behind us."

"Things are never as simple as we wish them to be. Life just doesn't work that way."

Emma heard a soft knock, and both of them looked up to see a man standing in the doorway. Emma thought it was another one of Wes's patients, but the look on his face suggested that it wasn't.

"Dr. Black, I am Mr. Davis. You seem surprised to see me. Did you not receive my message?"

"I was told I had received a letter, but it is with my other correspondence. I neglected to open it."

"It was just to notify you of my plan to visit. If you are busy right now, I can come back in an hour."

"No." He stood and motioned to the chair in front of his desk. "Please, sit down. This has gone on long enough."

The man glanced at Emma, and she looked at Wes, utterly confused.

"Emma, this man is Mr. Davis, a private investigator. Mr. Davis, this is Miss Emma Cooke."

The man's eyes widened. "Are you sure you don't want me to come back?"

"No. Clearly you are delivering this information in person because it is important. Emma, I hired an investigator to discover the truth behind your inheritance the day after I learned of it. Since his news pertains to you, I think you should be here to learn what he has uncovered."

Mr. Davis nodded. "I cannot give you a reason the house was left to Miss Cooke. But I can tell you that Miss Cooke wasn't always Miss Cooke."

CHAPTER NINE

Yea, mine own familiar friend, in whom I trusted, which did
eat of my bread, hath lifted up his heel against me.
—Psalm 41:9

Wes froze in his spot as dread flooded his body. It was too good to be true after all. She was too good to be true.

"What do you mean, I haven't always been Miss Cooke?"

"You were born Emmaline Eastman."

Eastman. *Eastman.*

He knew the name well. It was as bad as it could be.

"Your father changed your name when you were four just after your mother passed away. Cooke was your mother's maiden name."

Emma shook her head, and Wes had to give it to her. She looked like she was in complete and utter shock. "Why would my father change my name? You must be mistaken. None of this makes sense."

"He changed his as well. Your father was born Jeremiah Eastman. The son of David Eastman, the most notorious con artist on the East Coast."

Emma recoiled as if she had been slapped. "That is not true. I don't have a grandfather. My father told me he died before I was born."

"He died only a few years ago. He was in prison for most of your life. His list of crimes is long, including fraud, stock manipulation,

and impersonating a congressman. He was especially adept at conning extremely wealthy people. He blended in with them, claimed to
be one of them, and used their trust to steal their money."

"That isn't true. I never met my grandfather. My father said he
didn't have any money. We never had any money. My father taught
music all his life."

"That part is more than likely true. There probably wasn't any
money. Eastman seemed to lose it as soon as he stole it."

"He got my uncle to invest with him years ago," Wes said quietly.
"He lost nearly all of his money. Eastman is a dirty word in the Prescott
family. He was an unrepentant snake and deserved to rot in prison."

"There has to be a mistake," Emma said, her eyes filling with
tears. "My father and I had nothing to do with that man."

"For what it is worth, Dr. Black, I couldn't find anything else
about Jeremiah. He seems to have cut ties with his father when he
was a young man. He went on to marry Susan Cooke, who was an
opera singer in New York. He spent most of his life teaching at private schools around the country until his death due to a heart condition six years ago. I believe he changed his name to escape the
notoriety of his father. However, I do find it a strange coincidence
that the granddaughter of the man who conned your family is now
suddenly receiving a large inheritance from your closest relative."

"I also find it a strange coincidence." He looked at Emma,
unable to reconcile that the woman he knew as sweet, kind, and
honest was related to the man who had betrayed his family. His
uncle had thought of Eastman as a friend. Took him in as family.
Included him in his world. Trusted him. Just as Wes trusted Emma.
"Too strange."

Wes turned to leave, but Emma grasped his arm. "Wes…" The tears streamed down her face. His heart shattered. She looked as broken as he felt. "I never lied to you."

He pulled away from her. "How can I trust you?"

He walked out of the room, out of the building, and kept walking. He wished he could turn back time. He wished he had never attempted to learn the truth.

Emma wasn't sure what to do with herself. The news of her grandfather's true identity was too much for her to process. She wanted to call the investigator a liar, but too much of his report rang true.

Her father had rarely mentioned his father or his childhood. He told her that her grandfather had left the family penniless, but now she knew it was much more than that. Still, she wasn't content to take some investigator's word for it. She made a trip to the library and looked through old newspaper articles.

There were many about David Eastman. Part of her wanted to read everything written about him, but another part was too heartsick to take in the words. His picture accompanied one of the articles. It was large, and clear enough for her to see that the man's features matched her father's. Both tall, both dark haired, both with strong angular features that made them handsome. Like father, like son, some would say. But Emma would have to disagree. Her father was kind and good. He never stole from anyone. He had worked hard to provide for them until the day he died.

Good could come from bad. She firmly believed that.

She left the library and went back to the house. Legally, it was hers, but she didn't want it. She wasn't even sure she wanted to stay in Hazardville anymore.

She knew she hadn't done anything wrong. But every time she walked out onto the porch, she would remember the evenings she spent there with Wes. Every time she walked into the kitchen, she would remember that it was the first place she saw him smile. Even church wouldn't be the same, because memories of him sitting beside her and singing hymns in his deep, soothing voice would invade her.

It was foolish to fall in love with your enemy. But as much as they'd tried to tell themselves they were, they had never been on the same side. And now the history between their families would be too much to overcome.

And they were still no further along than they had been when this all began. They still didn't know why his aunt Virginia had decided to leave her house to a poor teacher she hardly knew.

A week had passed since Wes had seen Emma. One long, miserable week. His life had gone back to the way it was before it had been upended by her. He worked. He went home. There was nothing else. No distractions. No happiness. No joy. Just emptiness again. At least he had been numb before, which was preferable to what he was feeling right now.

He continued to visit Mr. Mercer every day. The old man was sitting up straight today with his arms crossed over his chest, and Wes felt like he had been called into the headmaster's office.

"Hello, Mr. Mercer."

"Don't you hello me, boy. Emma came over today to tell me she wasn't going to be able to visit me anymore."

"Did she say why?"

"She said she was going to be moving out of Hazardville. She has an interview with a school in Boston. One of her professors recommended her for the position."

"She's leaving?" He shook his head. "That isn't possible." He had gone through this week without seeing her, but that didn't mean he didn't want to see her. That he didn't hope for a glimpse of her while he was in town.

"Why isn't it possible? What is keeping her here? Clearly not you. You don't want to marry her."

"Of course I want to marry her. I'm in love with her."

"Oh?" He tilted his head and studied Wes. "Have you told her that?"

"No. It's all such a mess."

"Explain it to me."

Wes pulled out a chair and sat across from the elderly man. "My aunt left Emma her house."

"I know that. The whole town knows that."

"But no one knows why. I was especially curious, since Emma was nearly a stranger to her, so I hired a private investigator. Her grandfather and my family have history. He is an enemy to us."

"What did he do?"

"He stole a large sum of money from my uncle when he was a young man."

"Did your uncle end up living on the street?"

"No."

"Did he have to sell his summer home? Or his fancy boat?"

"No, but—"

"But what? 'For the love of money is the root of all evil: which while some coveted after, they have erred from the faith, and pierced themselves through with many sorrows.' It's just money. A man who chooses a fifty-year grudge over love is a foolish one."

"It is no coincidence that my aunt left her the house. Am I just supposed to ignore the mystery?"

"Yes." He nodded. "It is simple. You weren't happy before Emma. You aren't happy after Emma. But you are happy *with* Emma. Choose happiness. Whatever the history was between your families has nothing to do with the two of you. You can't honestly tell me you think she had anything to do with your aunt giving her the house. Have you seen the way she looks at you?"

He missed the way she looked at him. He missed the sound of her voice. Her laughter. Her smile. He missed *her*. There was a deep emptiness left by her absence, and he wasn't sure it could be filled again.

"I hurt her. I'm not sure I can get her back."

"The only way to find out is to try. Now stop bothering this old man and go find that girl before she leaves town for good."

Emma opened the window, needing to breathe some fresh air. Normally, she wouldn't be in her bedroom at this time of day, but she had barely left the house these past few days. It was hard to face the world. It wasn't shame she was feeling over her revealed history. She had led a good life. She had been raised by a good man, and while she was hurt that her father was so ashamed of his past that he went to the grave with the secret, she understood why he changed their names.

Yet she couldn't force herself to see and be seen by people. Her heart felt too heavy. She couldn't fake a smile or exchange pleasantries. Her heartbreak was too obvious. Mary had returned from her trip to Boston, and as soon as she saw Emma, she knew immediately something was wrong.

All this was her own fault. She should have kept her distance. Resisted the pull she felt toward Wes. Because she didn't, she was going to have to leave Hazardville. She had spent most of her life anonymously in big cities across the country. She couldn't stay anonymous here. She was a part of the community. The entire town probably knew the news by now. And while Mary assured her that no one would ever say anything against her, the doubt lingered in her mind.

She realized how outlandish it sounded. There was no logical reason why a wealthy woman would leave her estate to the grandchild of the man who had swindled her family. Emma would think there was something nefarious about it too.

Her interview with the school in Boston wasn't for another week or so. She would stay in the house until then. After that, she wasn't sure what she was going to do with it. Selling it seemed out of the question. Leaving it unlived in seemed like a crime. Maybe she would have the keys delivered to Wes before she left town. *Let him deal with it.*

She turned away from the window and tripped over the corner of the rug. She caught herself against the wall, but there was something about the sound that came from her hands hitting the wall that was different. It was a hollow sound. She knocked on the wall. Same hollow sound. The house was elaborately built. Complete with a turret that made the home seem even more grand. Emma thought it was just for show.

She walked out of the bedroom, studying the wall closely as she walked to the spot opposite from where she'd knocked. It was wallpapered with an intricate yet understated pattern. She had walked down this hallway more times than she could count, and today was the first time she noticed that there was a seam in the wall where a small, decorative table sat. There was always a vase filled with flowers there, so Emma had never bothered to look more closely at it. But today she did. Today she moved the vase. Behind it was a small keyhole.

It appeared she had found a secret door.

∞ CHAPTER TEN ∞

Be kindly affectioned one to another with brotherly love;
in honour preferring one another.
—*Romans 12:10*

Wes rushed over to Emma's house after he left Mr. Mercer. He wasn't sure he could go back to thinking of it as his aunt's home. This place would always be tied to Emma in his mind. It was the first place he had seen her. The first place where they had spoken. This house was where he first started to fall in love with her. With her hair falling out of its pins and flour smeared on her cheeks.

He rushed up the steps and knocked on the door. He expected to see Caroline, but Mary opened the door instead. She crossed her arms over her chest when she saw him.

"I was wondering how long it would take you to show up." She was clearly upset with him. She had every right to be.

"Is Emma here? I need to speak to her."

"Whether she is here or not depends on what you are planning to say to her. I will not let you hurt my friend again, Dr. Black. I don't care what your investigator told you. Emma is no criminal. She doesn't even want this house, and she wants to prove it so much, she is planning to leave here. It is your fault. She has no family, but here she has found friends and community, and because of some ancient grudge of yours she's going to leave everything behind."

"I was a fool. I don't want her to leave. I'm here to fix it."

"If you make her cry—"

"Mary?" He heard Emma's voice. "Who are you talking to?"

She appeared behind Mary. The hurt that flashed in her eyes was clear. Her expressions always gave away everything. Her anger, her fear, her hurt, her joy. How could he have ever thought that she had even the smallest part in whatever was going on? "Please, don't leave," he blurted out.

Mary walked away, leaving them alone.

"I'm not going just yet. Do you remember the key I asked you about?"

His head spun for a second, his thoughts trying to catch up to her words. "Yes. You said you couldn't find the door it goes to."

"I believe I found it. I think your aunt had a secret room built."

A secret room? "Have you been inside yet?"

"No. You have come just in time. We need to explore it."

"Are you sure you want me to accompany you?"

She was quiet for a moment, seeming to weigh her options. "It could be nothing. Or it could be everything we've been searching for. We have gone through every step of this together. Why stop now?"

"Promise me something before we go."

Her eyes narrowed suspiciously. "What?"

"Whatever the outcome, this ends today. The house is yours. It doesn't matter why or how it became yours. Hazardville is your home. You are loved here. No one wants you to leave. Most of all, I don't want you to leave. But if you do choose to leave, I will follow you wherever you go."

She looked at him for a moment, and he thought the corners of her lips almost turned upward into a smile. But she just nodded and moved to lead the way.

He followed her up the stairs to the second floor. He had only been up there once or twice. It was clear that his aunt hadn't overlooked a single detail when designing this home. From the window coverings to the rugs on the floor, every inch was tastefully done. He would have never noticed the seam in the wall that somehow perfectly lined up with the pattern in the wallpaper.

"This is brilliant," he said in awe as he ran his hand over it.

"This vase was very cleverly placed. It hides the keyhole."

Without another word from her, he picked up the table and moved it out of the way. Emma took the key out of her pocket and placed it in the lock.

It fit.

And with one turn of the key, the door swung open to reveal an empty room.

Emma walked into the room, Wes close behind her. "It's empty," she said as disappointment filled her once again.

"There must be something in here," Wes said as he stepped in front of her. "My aunt wouldn't keep an empty room locked." The room was small, circular in shape, barely big enough to hold a desk and a chair. It must have been built for storage.

"I see only a mirror."

"Exactly. Why would someone hang a mirror in an empty room that is barely big enough to hold two people?" He took the mirror off the wall. Emma expected to see a safe behind it, but there was only the nail that the mirror hung on. She turned to look at Wes, and an envelope attached to the back of the mirror caught her attention.

"There's something." She pulled the envelope off and opened it, her hands shaking as she did so. "It's addressed to me."

"Of course it is," he said, placing his hand on her shoulder. "Read it to me. If you want to, that is." She nodded.

"'My dearest Emma, if you have found this letter, you are as smart and as tenacious as I always suspected you were. I'm sure you have questions. Possibly dozens of them, so I'll get to the point. You probably think we are strangers. I am a stranger to you, but you are no stranger to me. A very long time ago, I fell in love with your father. We planned to marry, but the circumstances of the families we were born into prevented that. Obeying my father was one of the biggest regrets of my life, but if I hadn't you wouldn't have been born.

"'You were your father's greatest joy. Everything he did was to better your life. He didn't want the shame of his father's crimes to follow you, so he changed your name to give you a fresh start. He never wanted you to find out about his father. It was something that he and I have disagreed about over the years. It is important for one to know their history, even if it is an unpleasant one.

"'Your father wasn't able to express his feelings through words, only music. But there are a few things I'm sure he would like you to know. He loved your mother deeply. She was a beautiful and kind woman, and he saw a lot of you in her. He thought you were brilliant, and his deepest wish was for you to accomplish whatever you wanted to in life. This is where I come in. Your father always knew that his heart condition would take him from this earth earlier than he would like. He didn't want you to be forced into a marriage to survive. He saved every penny he could to give you a college education but, in the end, it was only enough to cover one year of tuition at Wesleyan University.

"'Your father had much pride, so I know it took a great deal for him to come to me for help. He asked me to look after you. I didn't want to interfere with your life, so I did it from afar. I paid for the rest of your schooling. That was my only intention at first. But when I suspected that I was ill, I wanted to make sure you would always be taken care of. It may be foolish of me, but I have come to think of you as my daughter. If I had ever had one, I would want her to be exactly like you. Intelligent. Independent. Strong. So I came to Hazardville, built this house for you, and recommended you for the job at Dixon Academy. It is my hope that you spend your life here, that you build the type of family that I used to wish for.

"'Now it is my turn to ask you for something. Look after my nephew. He can be a hard man sometimes, but he is deeply compassionate, loyal, and kind. When I saw him gazing at you at Christmas, I decided to come up with this little mystery in the hopes of bringing you two together. If I know my nephew, he will not rest until he learns why I have given you this house. And if he is as smart as I know him to be, he will find out that you are exactly what he needs to complete his life. I sincerely believe he will make a good husband (with a little training, that is).

"'This could backfire tremendously, but I think it will not. You may wonder why I chose to spend my last days on a small island away from everyone I know. It is because this is where your father and I dreamed of running away to and spending the rest of our days. I wanted to fulfill the one wish he had for himself. It helps me to feel closer to him. Please take care of yourself, Emma. Please be happy. Please love and be loved. Virginia Prescott.'"

They were silent for a long moment. Emma was having a hard time absorbing everything she had just read.

She felt Wes's thumb on her cheek, wiping away the tears that she hadn't realized were falling. "I imagine her having great fun putting all this into motion," he said softly.

"I can't believe she did all this for me." She looked up at him, her eyes so filled with tears that her vision was blurry.

"When you love someone, you want them to have the world. She loved you because she loved your father."

"I wish she had told me. I wish I could have known her. I have been so alone since my father died. Why didn't she come to me then?"

"I suspect she didn't want to make things harder on you than they already were. She would have had to reveal a secret your father never wanted you to know."

"But I found out anyway."

"You needed to know. We needed to know. We couldn't start out our life with that hanging over our heads."

"Our life?"

"Yes. That is, if you will have me. I love you, you know. I think I feared how fast I fell for you. I was a stupid, miserable man, and I am sorry for the way I have treated you. If I have learned anything this past week, it is that I am at my best when I am with you. I never want to be without you again. I came here to tell you that. Will you forgive me?"

She leaned into him, wrapping her arms around him, savoring the feeling of his arms curling around her. "I didn't want to fall in love with you."

"But you do love me?"

"Yes. Of course I love you. God brought us together, working through your aunt, who was my angel on earth."

He kissed her forehead before resting his chin on her hair. "Do you think Pastor Barker is at the church now?"

"Probably. Why?"

"We need to tell him that we want to get married as soon as possible."

"Dr. Black, is that a proposal?"

"Yes." He grinned at her. "Probably a poor one."

He dropped to his knee. "Emma Cooke, will you do me the honor of making me the happiest man in Hazardville by being my wife?"

"Of course." She tugged on his hand. "Now get up. We have a minister to find."

They ran out laughing together, and Emma couldn't help but think that she was about to have the greatest joy living in the house that love built.

ALL FOR LOVE

by

GAIL KIRKPATRICK

If we really want to love we must learn how to forgive.

—Mother Teresa

◌ Chapter One ◌

Present Day

She must be dreaming. Sara Loomis double-checked the address the estate lawyer gave her against the address in front of her. Yep, they matched. A week ago she was living in a one-bedroom apartment—granted, by choice—in Washington State. After all, it was just her. Not even a dog or a cat to take up space. Now she was the owner of a three-story Victorian in Hazardville, Connecticut, courtesy of her late maternal grandparents.

Looking up at the mansion, she shook her head. She was going to need to leave a breadcrumb trail to find her way around. But she loved it. From the stone base, to the wraparound deck, to the second-floor balcony, to the turret. It was hard to believe her mom grew up in this place. It was about as different as she could get from the one-story ranch-style house she'd called home as a child. Sara had never visited New England or met her grandparents. Once in a while, her mom would talk about home, always with love and a trace of sad regret. Of course, Sara asked why they didn't visit, but her mom just said "that bridge was burned."

Her parents had died five years ago while skiing when they were trapped by an avalanche. Her grandmother passed away six months ago, and her grandfather followed last month. They'd made one last attempt to mend that bridge by leaving the house and all of its contents to Sara, their only heir. She'd discovered this a mere two weeks ago when their lawyer found her. Her friends thought she was crazy to pack up and move across the country to a place she'd never been and where she didn't know a single living soul. But she looked at it as a grand adventure. A chance to get to know her grandparents, albeit in a secondhand way.

She took another look around the quiet street at all the tidy yards bathed in shade from the tall trees. It was a peaceful place. A place she could learn to call home.

Maybe here she could settle in, settle down, and figure out what to do with her life. Thankfully, her parents left her a tidy sum, so she could take her time, try a few things, and not be forced to settle for a career she disliked. Maybe this recent event was the Lord's way of telling her she'd simply been in the wrong place until now. She wasn't sure, but she was willing to give Hazardville and the people of Connecticut a chance.

So far, they seemed like a good sort.

Someone had mowed the yard and watered the potted flowers hanging along the wraparound porch. She could see where a swing used to be. Maybe it was stored in the garage. The paint was fresh and free from dirt or mildew. The screen door opened on silent hinges. All signs the house was cared for and loved.

As she stepped through the front doors and into total chaos, she revised her opinion. *Oh wow.* Either a hurricane had whipped through the place, or her grandfather was a complete and utter slob.

Drawers hung open from the entryway table. Papers littered the floor. Coats from a nearby open closet lay tossed onto the ground.

The living room furniture sat at odd angles, with the rug shoved against the wall. A giant, flat-screen TV sat atop a cherrywood credenza, so she didn't think someone robbed the place. However, the doors were open, and papers, books, cords—everything—lay scattered across the hardwood floor.

Sara hesitated before exploring any further, afraid to see if the rest of the house was in the same condition. While she might not have known her grandparents, she knew her mother had been a neat freak. Everything had a place. *Use it, put it back.* Her mom's words rang in her head, still to this day. The overwhelming urge to clean made her skin itch. Perhaps Royal Moffitt had been the opposite, or perhaps after he'd lost his wife, Marian, he'd quit caring. Grief did that. She knew from firsthand experience. Either way, she couldn't live in chaos. Even though her eyes burned and all she wanted to do was sleep after the long drive, she needed to, at least, put this room and the entryway back to order before she went to bed and, hopefully, slept for a solid fourteen hours. Besides, what better way to get to know her family than by exploring the house and learning what mattered most to them.

But first, if she was going to have the energy and strength to tackle three stories of mayhem, she better stock up on food and coffee. Lots of coffee.

As Sara climbed into her car, she made a quick call to the lawyer. While she didn't think someone had broken into the house—who leaves behind a flat-screen?—a warning in her gut told her something was off. The administrative assistant took a message and promised Ms. Aguirre would get back to her soon. A short drive down what appeared to be the main road produced several grocery store options, none of which were chains familiar to Sara. She picked the one closest to the house and stocked up on the essentials—bread, eggs, milk, coffee and French vanilla creamer, ice cream, and, of course, chocolate. As she was driving home, she spotted the Hazard Coffee House and had to stop. While she'd bought her own, she needed fresh, hot coffee and caffeine now.

Outside, there were a couple of cute wrought iron bistro tables and chairs and several planters of flowers inviting customers to hang out and enjoy their brew. Inside, Sara took a deep breath and stopped. *Wait. Do I smell garlic?* Was that a secret New England coffee thing? She wasn't sure she was brave enough to try it.

At the counter, a young woman about her age wiped the surface as she smiled and greeted Sara. "Hi, welcome to Hazard Coffee House. What can I get for you?"

"Before I order, I have to ask. Do you put garlic in your coffee or offer garlic pastries?" She'd noticed a few scrumptious-looking muffins and Danishes on the counter, but she was a little hesitant about choosing one just yet.

The woman, Julie, by her name tag, groaned. "I told you, Thad," she said, looking over at a rather cute man sitting at a corner table. The guy didn't respond, his focus on the laptop in front of him. Julie turned back to Sara. "I promise, there's no garlic in our coffee or baked goods. Just pure deliciousness. This used to be a pizza place. Well, it was a string of pizza places that couldn't stay in business. When I bought the house next door, this building came with it, and I tried something different."

"So how goes it?" Sara asked, hopeful she might have found her new favorite coffee shop on her very first day.

"Good. We've been open for three months, and business is steady."

"Could be better," the guy grumbled.

"Don't mind him. That's my brother, Thad, and my"—she cleared her throat—"*silent* partner. Are you new to town, or just passing through?"

"Brand-new." Sara laughed. "I just arrived this morning, and I live about two blocks away. And since you don't put garlic in your coffee, can I have an extra-large with French vanilla creamer, two sugars, and a cheese Danish to go?"

"Good choices. Decaf or regular? Most people switch to decaf after noon, but not me." After Sara replied, Julie got out the Danish and slipped it into a small paper bag before turning to fill the to-go cup with Sara's requested regular brew.

When she handed it to her, Sara took a quick whiff. "If it tastes as good as it smells, I'll definitely be a regular. I might even be back today. I picked up coffee at the store but forgot to check what kind of coffee maker I have."

"You don't know what kind of coffee maker you have?" Julie's raised eyebrows made Sara laugh again. Yeah, most people should know that kind of thing.

"I just inherited a house from my grandparents. The place is a disaster. I didn't even make it as far as the kitchen before I decided I better do a supply run. And the house is enormous. Three stories. I'm hoping the entire house isn't trashed like the living room and entryway."

"Sounds like one of the houses on School Street," Julie said.

"It is. My grandparents were the Moffitts, but I never met either of them."

Thad, who'd been lost in his computer work, joined them at the counter. He was tall, at least in comparison to Sara's meager five foot one. He had dark brown hair with a few streaks of gray shining through and dark brown eyes with pretty flecks of gold. But it was his smile that caught her attention. It was like a summer day full of sunshine.

"The Moffitts on School Street?" he asked.

"Did you know them?" Her stomach did a quick loop the loop. At last, someone who might be able to tell her about her family.

"I did, and I'm so sorry for your loss. They were wonderful, caring people who loved each other very much."

While his words filled her soul with delight, they also tore at her heart. They sounded like grandparents she would have loved to have grown up with. It also made her more than curious why her mom stopped talking to them. She'd resigned herself years ago to the fact that she'd never find the answer. "Thank you. Can I ask how you knew them?"

"Sorry, I forgot to introduce myself. I'm Thad Jackson. Besides being my sister's not-so-silent *silent* partner, I have a handyman business. I've worked for your grandparents several times."

"Really? Can I ask a weird question then?" At his nod, Sara continued. "Was my grandfather messy?"

Thad chuckled. "Um, no. He was anything but. I'd call him fastidious. Obsessively so. He used to clean up as I worked. I heard you say the house is a mess, which makes no sense. I was there a few days before he passed away, fixing a loose step on the back stairs. The place was as pristine as ever."

"Well, it's not now. At least, not in the two rooms I saw. I called their lawyer, but she hasn't returned my call. Do you know of anyone else who might have been inside the house? The lawyer said I was the only direct heir and named person in the will."

"They might have hired someone to tend the yard or clean inside, but it sounds as though the person did the opposite," Julie suggested. "I haven't heard of any break-ins in the area recently. Have you, Thad?"

"No, I haven't, and you would have been the first person I'd have checked on." He turned his attention and the full force of those concerned brown eyes on Sara. "Were there any other signs someone might have broken in?"

"The lawyer said someone from the church cleaned out the food when they couldn't find me right away and donated it. As for other signs, I didn't go through the entire house yet. It's not like I'd know if anything is missing."

"That makes sense. Do you want me to come look around? I've been in most of the rooms at one point or another doing repairs." Thad's warm, sincere eyes had Sara hoping the house needed more repairs. She wouldn't mind an excuse to get to know Thad Jackson better, but she wouldn't take him away from his work for a nonsensical reason either.

"Honestly, I don't think anyone broke in. There's still a huge flat-screen TV in the living room. Let's wait for their lawyer to call back before we jump to the worst-case scenario."

"You're welcome to wait here if you feel uncomfortable alone at the house," Thad said.

She'd thought about it. What if it was a crime scene? If so, she shouldn't be cleaning stuff up. But unless Ms. Aguirre had an inventory list, how would anyone know? Besides, if she didn't feel safe during the day, there was no way she'd feel comfortable at night. Better to find out now. "Thanks, but I've got ice cream in the car."

"If you need anything, anything at all, just ask," Thad offered.

✎⌾ CHAPTER TWO ⌾✎

Sara grabbed the two bags of groceries and bounded up the front steps, eager to get started on cleaning. After she explored her new home, of course. She pushed the front door open and took a moment to guess which direction would lead to the kitchen. She probably should have checked that out that before her supply run. Following the hallway, she entered the dining room. Also a mess. *Great.* Off to the right was another room, most likely a family room or, once upon a time, the parlor. She had no clue except, based on all the bookshelves, it looked like her grandparents used it for a reading room. Bookshelves that were empty because the contents were on the floor. She was going to need a lot more coffee.

Straight across from where she stood was another door, which led finally to the kitchen. This room wasn't in the same shape as the rest of the house. In fact, it looked untouched except for a few open cabinets. She took a moment to look around. There was a powder room off to the left, stairs leading up, and a breakfast nook in the back. At some point the room had been updated with marble counters, smooth cabinet doors painted white, and gleaming stainless-steel appliances.

Sara unloaded the groceries then turned to explore. As the lawyer stated, the cabinets were devoid of food, but she had dishes and cookware. And, thank goodness, a coffee maker that matched the coffee she'd purchased. Under the kitchen sink were cleaning products. A peek out the back window showed a lovely deck to greet the morning sun and a yard to make a gardener weep for joy. Sara wasn't a gardener, but it looked like she needed to up her game and learn not to kill off plants just by looking at them.

A creak from upstairs had her pausing in her tracks. A chill ran through her body. All her attention zeroed in on that noise. She rubbed her arms then laughed at herself. Old houses creaked all the time. It meant nothing. She continued her exploration, reaching the exit to the deck. Her hand no sooner landed on the knob than the door swung open at her touch.

She froze in place, gaze glued on the lock. The damaged lock. She tried not to breathe as she listened to the surrounding sounds. Outside, a bird tweeted away. The air conditioner hummed in the corner, and there... There it was again. A board on the upper floor creaking as if complaining about the weight suddenly pressing down on it. But where upstairs?

She pulled her phone out of her pocket and took slow, silent steps through the dining room. The smart thing would be to return to the coffee shop and call the police, and that's what she was going to do. But just as she reached the front staircase, about five feet from the door and safety, a crash overhead had her heart and feet stopping. She wanted to run, but her body wasn't listening. Air built up in her lungs, which were threatening to burst.

Why hadn't she taken Thad up on his offer?

Feet pounded overhead. Another crash, followed by a thud. The person was heading toward the back staircase. If she didn't move, whoever it was would see her. *Should I run for the car? Yes. No. What if they run that way for a quicker getaway?* They might catch her before she made it inside her car. She ran to the living room. Pressed against a wall where she couldn't be seen from either entrance, she held her breath and sent up a silent prayer. The kitchen door crashed against a wall. She ran to the rear of the house, hoping to catch a look at the intruder. But by the time she got to the kitchen window, all she could see was a glimpse of someone going over the wooden fence.

She hit 911 as she slammed the back door, grabbed a kitchen chair, and tucked it under the doorknob. Then she hurried to the front, locked the door, pulled it shut, and ran for her car. She hit the locks and ducked down low. She gave the dispatcher her name and address and reported the break-in. They promised officers would be there in a matter of minutes and then hung up. *Huh. Not like on TV. Where was the calm, caring operator who stayed on the phone until help arrived?*

In what seemed like forever but was only about three minutes, sirens pierced the air, allowing Sara to take her first real breath. When the officer arrived, he came to her driver's window. Sara repeated to him what she'd told the 911 operator. He took her house key and told her to stay put. He didn't have to tell her twice.

A second officer joined him. First, they walked the perimeter of the house, each going in a different direction and meeting back at the front door. She didn't know what happened once they entered, and she wasn't about to get out to see. To calm her nerves and pass the time, she sent a text to her best friend, Doreen, in Washington.

Arrived safely. Love the house. It's a mansion, well, a three-story Victorian. But...

Here she paused for a moment. Should she tell her about the break-in? Doreen would probably tell her it was a sign she shouldn't have moved to Connecticut. But she'd also worry needlessly for her friend. That was Doreen. She had the biggest heart on the planet.

Three little dots showed up on the screen, followed by Doreen's response.

BUT WHAT?

I JUST MISS YOU. PROMISE YOU'LL COME VISIT SOON.

PROMISE. I PUT IN FOR VACATION THIS MORNING. BE THERE IN TWO MONTHS. HAVE A ROOM READY FOR ME. HUGS.

Before Sara could respond, the officers exited through the front door. At their signal, she got out of the car and joined them on the front porch.

"The house is empty now," one of them said. "Looks like they broke in through the kitchen door. Do you know if they stole anything?"

She shrugged. "Honestly, no. I just took possession of the place this morning. I inherited it from my grandparents."

"I'm sorry for your loss. We'll file a report. If you find damage or something missing, you can follow it up with your insurance. Normally, this is an extremely safe neighborhood."

"It doesn't seem like it to me." The urge to laugh and cry at the same time swept over her. Probably an adrenaline crash.

"We're betting it was a random hit. Someone taking a chance with an empty house. We'll have a patrol drive by tonight."

The officer advised her to fix the broken lock as soon as possible, took down her personal details, and wished her a good day.

After they drove off, Sara took a deep breath before heading inside. The first thing she did was lock the front door behind her.

She then double-checked the kitchen door to make sure the chair was still in place under the doorknob. Spotting Thad Jackson's business card on the refrigerator, she called him. Five minutes later, the doorbell rang.

Thad was in the middle of fixing a secondhand espresso machine for his sister when the call came. He tossed his tools in his box and told Julie he'd be back later. Thad had hoped to see Sara again. There had been something in her eyes that captured his attention. It made him want to get to know her better, but he wished it could be under different circumstances. It was a short drive from the coffee shop to the Moffitt place, but he needed to make a quick stop for supplies. After picking up a new lock set at the hardware store, he pulled up in front of the School Street house and did a double take. *What is she doing here?*

He grabbed the bag and his toolbox and headed up the front walk. Sara held a plate of cookies as the two women talked. The older woman took one look at him and said goodbye.

She met Thad's eyes as they passed. "Thaddeus."

"Mrs. Newington." Thad stepped aside, shaking his head in confusion. He couldn't think of one good reason why she'd stop by. He turned his attention back to Sara, noting that despite the situation, she smiled and held the plate out to him.

"Cookie?"

He glanced at the offered goods. The smell of peanut butter and chocolate tickled his senses. Tempting, but he declined. "Mind if I ask what she was doing here?"

"Mrs. Newington?" Sara's brows pulled down, creating tiny lines over her pretty hazel eyes. "She's a neighbor who wanted to welcome me to town and give her condolences on my grandparents' passing. Why?"

Thad gave one more look over his shoulder as he followed Sara inside. "She was no friend of your grandparents."

"Really? She told me she and my grandmother loved to bake together."

That had Thad laughing. "As far as I know, they never baked together. They competed against each other every year at the Four Town Fair. Your grandmother beat her out every time. I wouldn't be surprised if she didn't break in here to steal Marian's prize-winning recipe for zucchini bread. It was that good."

Sara stopped in her tracks, blocking his entrance into the house as she spun around to face him. "A recipe? That's the most ridiculous thing I've ever heard of. Who trashes the living room and not the kitchen to steal a recipe?"

"Someone who's tired of losing and figures it would be well hidden. Your grandmother had offers from a couple of bakeries to buy the rights to her recipe, you know."

"I can see your point. However, I don't think it was Mrs. Newington. Whoever broke in here could get over the six-foot fence in the backyard. She didn't look capable of that."

Thad agreed it wasn't likely that Mrs. Newington, who was closer to sixty than fifty, had jumped over the fence. Still, he didn't trust her welcoming committee act. Sara continued into the house, and as Thad got his first look at the mess, his feet slowed to a complete stop. He'd done work for Royal and Marian Moffitt for years. They were his first customers when he'd started his business at sixteen. He'd never seen the house anything less than spotless. A whirlwind would have created less of a mess.

"Wow."

Sara paused for a moment before heading to the kitchen. "Yep. Let me know if you notice anything missing."

He glanced around, being careful not to step on the debris. It was hard to say at the moment. He'd offer to do a walkthrough after she cleaned up. In the kitchen, he noticed everything looked normal except for the chair under the doorknob. As he got to work inspecting the damage, Sara asked if music would bother him while he worked. He shook his head, and she took out her phone and swiped the screen. He wasn't sure what type of music he expected. Current pop? Or even a little old-school country. Instead, Christmas carols filled the air. In the middle of June.

As Thad worked to replace the back door lock, Sara slipped off to what the Moffitts called the reading nook. She sang carols—often off-key—as she picked up books. Adorable, and he couldn't seem to wipe the grin off his face as he worked.

When he finished with the door lock, he inspected the latches on all the ground-floor windows and the front door. He didn't get it. He'd lived in Hazardville his whole life. They didn't get home invasions. And this person didn't just break into the house. They trashed the place. He had a bad feeling that whatever they were looking for, they didn't find it and might return.

"The back door's fixed," he said, joining her to pick up books. "I checked the windows. They've got good locks, and they're triple paned, which will make it harder for someone to break. The front door lock is also good and sturdy."

"Thank you. I can't tell you how much I appreciate how fast you came over. I feel safer already."

"Well, while the doors and windows will be harder to break into now, if the thief is determined, they'll find a way. I recommend getting a security system. I brought it up a couple of times to your grandfather, but he said they'd never needed one before, so why put one in."

Thad could see the logic—at the time. But times changed, and he was sure if Royal Moffitt knew his granddaughter might be in danger, he wouldn't hesitate to put in a system.

"That's a great idea. Do they take a long time to install?"

"Not really. I've got a buddy who installs them. Let me call him."

Thad stepped away for a few minutes to call his friend. He explained the size of the house and the number of access points and answered his friend's questions before hanging up.

"Good news and bad news," he said. At Sara's questioning look, he continued. "My friend knows the perfect system for you and can install it in a day. The bad news is, it's out of stock right now. He's expecting a delivery next week."

"Oh." Sara glanced around, twisting her fingers together. "I guess that's okay. The police thought it was a random attempt and now that the thief knows the house isn't empty, they won't be back."

"Maybe, but I'd feel better with you here alone with some kind of deterrents. I don't suppose you have a big, loud dog, do you?"

Sara laughed, making her eyes sparkle. "No, I don't. I used to live in a one-bedroom apartment. Not exactly the best environment for dogs. Especially big ones. I've been thinking about it though. We always had dogs when I was growing up, but losing my last one, Bear, gutted me."

"Well, when you're ready. Until then, how would you feel if I were to install motion-sensor lights on the back of the house, the driveway, and the front of the house, along with door alarms?"

"That sounds like a great compromise. Do you have time to do it today?" Her shoulders tensed up, and he was almost certain she was holding her breath as she waited for his answer. He'd have to bounce a few things around, but he'd make it work. Besides, it would give him a little more time to get to know his new neighbor.

"Sure. I'll even install it all at no charge. I owe that much to your grandparents. You can think of it as a welcome gift."

"Thad, you don't have to do that." Pink stole over her cheeks, reminding him of a sunrise.

"I know, but I want to."

"That's really nice of you. Thank you—" Before she could say more, a knock at the front door cut her off. Sara hesitated before walking out of the room. Thad wasn't sure if there was something else she wanted to say or if she was afraid to find out who was knocking. He followed her at a distance, not to eavesdrop but for safety.

Sara opened the door to a man Thad had never seen before. "Hello. Can I help you?"

The man stood with his hands stuffed in his jeans pockets and his shoulders pulled in. "Uh, yeah. Sorry, this is awkward. I didn't mean to drop in unannounced, but I didn't have a number to call."

"No worries." Sara glanced over her shoulder at Thad, her eyes wide and round. He wasn't sure if the look was code or not, but he moved closer to the door and into the guy's line of sight. For a first day in a new place, Sara sure got a lot of visitors. Guess word had gotten around of her arrival. Small towns.

The visitor's gaze met his, and the guy flinched. Weird. It wasn't like he'd shot the guy a dirty look or anything. "You've got company. I can come back later."

As he turned to go, Sara stepped outside. "Wait. Who are you?"

He paused. "I'm your cousin, Billy Bischoff."

"What?"

"I just wanted to give my condolences. Your grandparents and I were really close. As a kid, I spent a lot of time with them and then toward the end. Maybe we can get together sometime and talk." His gaze darted to Thad, who had moved to the doorway, and then back to Sara. The guy—Billy—flashed her a smile, but in Thad's opinion, it looked forced.

"Now's not a good time, but I'd like that."

Sara and Billy exchanged phone numbers as Thad walked back to the living room window where he could watch as Billy left. He didn't care for the guy. There was something in his manner that didn't come across as authentic. When Billy reached the sidewalk, he turned around, his gaze on the upper levels of the house. What was he looking at? After a few seconds, he kept going down the street. Sara joined Thad at the window.

"Isn't that great? I've got a cousin. My lawyer must have told him I was here. So cool. I have family again. I can't wait to hear his stories." With that, she headed back to the reading room and her cleanup.

Thad stayed at the window watching, running Billy's words through his mind. The guy claimed to have spent a lot of time with the Moffitts at the end, but Thad had never seen him before or heard of him.

✍ Chapter Three ✍

What a crazy first day. Thad had just left for the second time after installing new motion-sensor lights and door alarms. He'd asked her to lock up the first floor and to open a window only if it didn't have easy access, was on the second floor, and if she was in that room. They were probably overreacting, but she couldn't deny she breathed easier.

She'd cleaned the entryway and the reading and living rooms. Fatigue swept through her entire body. Muscles she didn't know she'd used ached. When her phone pinged with a message, it sounded like a good excuse to sit down and take a break. She dropped into a wingback chair in the reading room that gave her a view into the living room and out to the front yard. She'd rather have sat on a porch swing and enjoyed the June weather, but she still needed to find and hang the swing. Not to mention get over the uneasy feeling of being watched.

Instead, she read the text from her best friend out west.

So, do you have my room ready yet? LOL. How was your first day?

Good. Found an amazing coffee shop just a few blocks away and...

Should she mention Thad and how cute he was? Or his kind eyes and how just being around him made her feel calm and safe?

No, it was too early, and Doreen would get her hopes up that she'd found someone new. Her best friend was the ultimate romantic. Doreen would tell her to just ask him out.

AND WHAT?

AND I THINK COMING HERE TO HAZARDVILLE WAS THE RIGHT CHOICE. I LOVE THE HOUSE. IT'S GORGEOUS. WILL SEND PICS SOON. ONE OF THE NEIGHBORS BROUGHT ME WELCOME COOKIES.

NICE!

I'VE ALREADY MADE A FRIEND WHO MAKES A GREAT CUP OF COFFEE AND I MIGHT HAVE MADE A SECOND FRIEND TOO.

Three red hearts appeared.

I'M HAPPY FOR YOU, BUT I MISS YOU. CAN'T WAIT TO SEE YOU. THE NEXT TWO MONTHS WON'T GO BY FAST ENOUGH. HAVE TO GO. HAVING DINNER WITH MY MOM. SEND THOSE PICS. HUGS.

Sara held her phone close as if she could feel her friend's hug coming through the line. She missed Doreen. She missed Washington and the mountains and evergreens, but she believed moving to Hazardville was the right choice. Her life had hit a lull and needed shaking up.

Something poked the back of her thigh. Must be a spring. She shifted on the chair to get comfortable as she felt along the cushion. She touched cold metal and pulled it out from between the cushion and the chair frame. Not a spring but a key.

Not just any key. A beautiful brass skeleton key. She held it up and looked around. What did it go to? Curiosity won out over exhaustion. She tried the doors on the main floor with no luck. Nor did it fit in the desk drawers. Strange. Why keep a key that fit nothing in its vicinity? And what was it doing tucked into the chair? Maybe it fell out of her grandfather's pocket?

The day had long slipped into night. Her multiple cups of coffee no longer fueled her body or mind. Sara shut off all but one small lamp in the reading room, double-checked that the locks were all engaged and the sensor lights were on, and headed up to bed. The only room besides the kitchen not trashed by her uninvited guest was the master bedroom. Thank goodness. Sara lay on top of the covers with the key still in her hand. She couldn't wait to show Thad in the morning.

What did it mean that he was her last thought of the day?

In the blink of an eye, the sun streamed through the bedroom windows as a bird tweeted at the top of his lungs. Sara blinked the sleep away, grabbed her phone and the key, and then stumbled down the back stairs to the kitchen. She needed coffee, stat.

As the nectar of life flowed into her cup, she pulled up the Connecticut Humane Society website to see what kinds of dogs they had for adoption. Bear had been such a comfort to her after her parents' death, but losing him had broken her heart, and she'd been afraid to adopt again. But maybe part of her new start here was also opening her heart to a new fur baby. Sadly, the organization had only two dogs listed, and both were noted as "adoption pending." Wonderful for the dogs, not so great for her, but she took it as a sign that neither were the right companion for her. She'd look again in a few days.

While she'd made a big dent in the mess the day before, she still had the dining room and the other bedrooms upstairs to clean. She was dying to show off her find to Thad and Julie, but priorities. She took the coffee into the dining room, set her cup on the table, and looked around.

A deep sigh escaped.

Whoever had broken in had had a field day.

The dining room had a built-in oak hutch with open shelves, doors, and drawers taking up a whole wall. She was thankful the culprit had just made a mess and had broken nothing in their frantic search of the house. She scooped up an armful of linens that she then dropped on the table before folding and putting them away. There were tablecloths, runners, and place mats for every holiday. Sara put the patriotic ones on top. She'd look later in storage for other holiday decorations, as Independence Day was just a few weeks away. As she went about her task, she moved a few crystal pieces around, satisfied with the progress she was making. She pulled the last stack of linen napkins closer, and her hand landed on a hard object.

She tossed a few cloths aside and discovered a red notebook. The intruder probably had been in such a hurry, he hadn't even seen the book. Or it held nothing of interest.

Sara dropped into the nearest chair.

The front of the notebook had the initials *MM* embossed in silver. Her grandmother. Sara ran a hand over the cover, letting her fingers trace the initials. She opened the book and sniffed the pages, catching a light lavender scent. Given she'd discovered the notebook in the dining room, she thought it might be a cookbook. Maybe even the one containing the award-winning zucchini bread recipe. But no, it was a journal dating back to when her mom was in her late teens.

Sara held the book against her heart. Should she read it? Part of her screamed yes! What better way to get to know her grandmother?

She might even learn what caused the great rift in her family. The other part whispered no. What if she read something horrible or humiliatingly personal?

After a few indecisive moments, she turned to page one. The summer when her mother was seventeen. She would have been getting ready to start her senior year of high school. A year before she met Sara's dad.

Her grandmother's handwriting was beautiful, with elegant loops. Sara forgot all about cleaning as she got lost in her grandmother's memories. She wrote about Sara's mom, Jessie, and what a wonderful child she was. Carefree, a bit mischievous, and always smiling. But then Jessie changed. As a teen she became distracted, quiet, spending more and more time alone in her "secret room."

"I wonder what that means? Her bedroom? No, she'd just say bedroom." Sara mused her thoughts out loud—not that anyone was there to respond, but it helped her process and not feel so alone. She picked up the skeleton key she'd found the night before. "Did I miss a room last night? Maybe a library?"

She set the journal down and tried all the doors again on the main floor, then the upper rooms. No luck. The key didn't fit in any of the doors.

She looked at her watch and realized it was almost lunchtime and she'd skipped breakfast. "Okay, a quick bite, then back to cleaning."

In the kitchen, as she nibbled on her favorite, tuna on toast, she continued reading. Some days earned multiple entries, while other entries were months apart. She flipped the page to the next entry, dated six months after graduation. Her mom should have been off to college. Sara already knew this wasn't what happened.

My greatest treasure—my daughter—is lost to me. It has been months with only a spare postcard here and there, each successive one telling me she's farther and farther from home.

Sara could hear the heartache in her grandmother's words, could see the dried tear stains on the page. Why had her mother cut her parents out of her life?

Her grandmother went on, but didn't answer her question.

There isn't a day goes by that I don't think of and miss my girl terribly. I received another postcard this morning. This one from Seattle. It had beautiful snowcapped mountains and tall evergreens. Jessie says they've found a place to rent and call home. Oh, what I wouldn't give to see my baby girl again. I suggested to Royal that we sell everything and move west to repair our family. He refused. He's such a proud man. It's not that he values these material possessions or house more than his daughter. He says she'll be back. I hope he's right. Until then, I have very little that brings me joy these days. I think about the priceless treasure some say this old house hoards. I'd gladly give it away if I could just make my family whole again.

Sara rubbed her palm over the hollow ache in the middle of her chest. She understood all too well what it was like to be left with nothing but memories of someone you loved. It seemed she and her grandmother had something in common. She closed the journal and placed it on the kitchen counter.

What treasure was her grandmother referring to?

The house had, from what Sara's untrained eye could determine, quality furniture and decor, but nothing struck her as "priceless." Could someone else have known what her grandmother was talking about? Could the burglar have been after this "treasure"? And if so, did they find it? Or would they be back?

Chills ran down Sara's spine.

I'd gladly give it away if I could just make my family whole again. Her grandmother's words whispered in her head. Having lost her parents and then her beloved pet, Sara could relate to how empty her grandmother's heart must have felt.

A bird outside chirped, its tune happy and melodic. Another responded. And then a sudden creak overhead had Sara nearly jumping out of her skin. She couldn't shake the chill. She felt as empty as the house, and it was imperative that she get out.

No one else was in the house. She knew that, but yet, that was the problem. She was tired of being alone. She grabbed her purse, the key, and the journal and headed to the only place she knew to go.

Thad finished carrying in the last of the day's supply delivery at the coffee shop. All morning long, he'd thought up excuses to go check on Sara. He hadn't liked the idea of her staying alone in her grandparents' house—well, hers now—after the break-in. He also knew suggesting she stay somewhere else crossed a line. His mother and sister had taught him to value and respect women, their intuition, and their strength. But that didn't mean he didn't worry.

He'd just decided he didn't need any excuse other than checking in and seeing how she was doing when the front bell jingled at the same time the oven buzzer went off. Julie asked him to handle the oven while she helped their customer.

"Hi there." Julie's cheerful voice carried to the kitchen. "You're back. Guess that means my coffee passed your approval?"

"Definitely. I've been cleaning all morning—mostly—and need a pick-me-up." Sara's voice warmed him from the inside out. Or maybe that was the oven. Either way, he was happy she'd come into the shop.

"Your timing is perfect. We're just taking a new test batch of scones out of the oven. Lemon blueberry. You can be my taste taster."

Thad took a moment to grab a ceramic plate and put a hot scone on it. He paused at the door as his gaze met Sara's. Her smile notched up a smidge, and he was almost certain he saw relief in her eyes.

"Oh wow. That smells amazing."

Julie stepped away to fix Sara's coffee and turned back with a fresh cup and a fork. Then she excused herself to tend to the kitchen, giving him a little nudge closer as she left him and Sara alone to talk. He'd have to do something nice for Julie later to thank her.

"Any issues last night?" he asked.

"No. Thankfully, it was a quiet and uneventful night. Or at least until this bird decided to put on a concert outside my bedroom window around six this morning." She rolled her eyes and took a long drink of coffee.

Thad chuckled. "Sounds like he let you sleep in. The ones near my place start around four thirty."

"Ugh. Feel free to keep them at your house." Sara snickered then bit down on her lip, seriousness washing over her. "Thank you again for your help yesterday. I'm not sure what I was expecting when I got here, but it definitely wasn't dealing with a break-in."

"No problem. That's what friends and neighbors are for."

She bit her lip again before looking up at him through dark, thick lashes. "Which are we? Friends or neighbors?"

"Technically, we're neighbors. Julie lives in the house next door to here, and I live just a few streets over." He knew she'd just arrived in town, but he felt like he'd known Sara forever. She was easy to talk with and to be around, and he very much wanted to be her *friend*. "Can I be honest?"

"Please do."

"Okay." Normally, he didn't put himself out there in the dating world. Most women left him tongue-tied and lost as to what to say. Sara was different. Maybe it was how strong she'd been yesterday after the break-in? Or maybe it was her warm, welcoming smile? Or that she sang Christmas carols in summer. Whatever it was, it gave him the courage to take a chance. "I like you, and I hope we can get to know one another better."

Pink swept over Sara's cheeks. "I'd like that too. You and Julie have been so nice to me. You're the first people I've met, and yet it feels like we've been friends for much longer."

Great. Did she just friend-zone him?

Before he could clarify, the front door opened. Sara took her coffee and scone and stepped to a nearby table, giving the next person room at the counter.

"Good afternoon, Mr. Dawson. What can I get for you today?" Julie asked as she swept back into the front of the store.

"How about a small black coffee and whatever smells so good?"

"Coming right up."

"Thaddeus, it's good to see you. How's business? And who's this lovely young lady?"

"Keeping me on my toes, thank you for asking. This is Sara Loomis. She just moved to Hazardville. Royal and Marian were her grandparents."

Mr. Dawson paused in reaching for his coffee as his head swung in Sara's direction. Sadness clouded his eyes. "Sara, it's so nice to meet you, finally."

"Finally?" she asked. Thad heard the shock in her voice and moved around the counter. He wanted to offer her some kind of support, which was crazy, as they'd known each other for a grand total of twenty-four hours. Somehow, in that short time, he'd already become protective of her.

"I've heard a lot about you over the years. Your grandparents were good friends of mine."

"But they never met me. How could they tell you about me?"

"Your mom wrote to your grandmother from time to time with updates on you and sometimes sent a school photo. Both your grandma and grandpa were so proud when you graduated from college."

Sara stood there, speechless, for a few moments. Then finally, she said, "I'm sorry, I didn't know. I wish I'd had a chance to meet them."

"I know they wanted that too. But sometimes, often, life doesn't give us what we want." Sorrow bordering on anger filled his voice, which surprised Thad. Mr. Dawson was usually very upbeat. In a more gentle voice he said, "Sara, I am truly sorry for your loss. If you need anything, please don't hesitate to reach out, and I hope I see you on Sunday at church. If you'll allow me, I'll share a few stories about your grandparents with you."

"Thank you, Mr. Dawson. That would be wonderful."

He reached for his coffee and scone. "Right now, I'm going to relax for a few minutes right over there. Then I need to get going. Can't start a softball game without the pitcher."

He moved to a table a few yards away and settled with his coffee, scone, and newspaper. Sara sat down at her table, her face void of all emotion.

"Are you okay?" Thad settled next to her.

"I think I'm just shocked. My mom never told me she talked to my grandparents or sent them letters and pictures of me. I wish she had talked to me more, but every time I brought up her parents, she shut down."

"That's got to be hard. At least living in their house you'll have time to learn about them a little, and I'm sure Mr. Dawson can tell you a lot."

"He seems nice."

"He's everyone's favorite PE teacher," Julie said from behind the counter, where she'd been filling the case with the new scones. "Or he was until he retired a few years ago. Not that you could tell. He's the star of the senior softball league and still coaches Little League."

Sara reached into her pocket and pulled out a skeleton key.

Thad held out his hand. "Can I see that?"

She handed it to him. "I found it last night, but can't find a door to match it. I also found my grandmother's journal. She talks about a priceless treasure. You wouldn't know anything about that, would you?"

A treasure? He'd been inside the Moffitt house countless times and had never seen or heard of a treasure. He knew them to be modest, humble people. "Sorry, I can't be of help there."

"No worries." Her gaze dropped to her coffee as silence filled the air.

"What do you think of the house?" Julie asked. "It must be wonderful to live in such a grand old place. All that history and space." His sister's eyes lit up. Not that he blamed her. Julie's place could comfortably house a single person, but anything beyond that would push it.

"The house is beautiful, and they've kept it in great shape, but I don't know. It doesn't feel like home yet. Not sure if it's because it's new to me or that there's too much space. My last place was a one-bedroom apartment. The house is really too big for one person."

"You could get a roommate or rent a few of the rooms out," Thad suggested.

"I guess. I'm not sure how I feel about living with strangers. I thought about getting a dog, or I might sell the house."

"Sell it?" Thad asked, a little shocked. She'd just arrived. Then again, she'd also been burglarized.

"It was just a thought. I honestly don't know what I'm going to do yet. I was thinking I'd like to get the original blueprints and see what history I could gather on the house first. If I did decide to sell, it could help. Or it might even qualify for the historic registry. I could turn it into a museum."

"I guess it couldn't hurt to have that information. If you want, I can drive you to the public records office and give you a quick tour of town."

"Yeah, the tour will take about five minutes," Julie said.

Sara laughed. "That sounds like a great idea. Maybe I'll even find a reason to stick around Hazardville." Her smile landed on Thad, and he hoped he might be the reason to keep her there.

"Hey, you never know." Julie clapped her hands. "Maybe you'll find out the house has a secret room or passageway that leads to a cave full of treasure."

Chapter Four

Thad parked his truck in the lot next to a multistory brick building with white columns framing the front. Together, they climbed the stairs, and Thad held the door open for her.

"Thank you for coming with me. I'm not taking you away from a work project, am I?"

"Not at all. It's my pleasure. Besides helping Julie bring in stock at the shop, my day was clear, and I'd rather spend the time with you. I know you haven't had the best first impression of Hazardville." He wouldn't blame her for selling the house and returning out west. "I'm hoping I can change your mind about us."

"It hasn't been all bad. I met Julie...and you." She flashed him a quick, sincere smile before shifting her gaze away. "Besides, we have petty crime in Washington too."

"Were you in Seattle?" He pointed to the town clerk's office and reached to open the door for her.

"No, I lived about an hour away from there, but my friends and I went to Seattle a lot. It's a fun city with a lot to do, even for the locals. I loved going to Pike Place Market."

"Is that the place where they toss the fish?" He'd never been out west, but he'd seen some fun videos of the city.

"The Pike Place Fish Market. They're kind of weird but entertaining to watch, and the fish is the best. So fresh."

Their conversation paused as Sara explained to the clerk that she was looking for the original blueprints to a house she just inherited. She gave the address and waited while the clerk looked the information up on the house. It would be cool if it had a secret room or passageway.

"You said School Street, correct?"

"Yes, that's right. It was owned by my grandparents, Royal and Marian Moffitt." Sara's voice broke at the end. He couldn't imagine what she was going through. He still had both of his parents, although he didn't speak to his dad often. His mother's parents were happily retired in New Mexico, and while he had lost his paternal grandparents in his teens, at least he'd gotten to know them.

Thad gave her hand a quick squeeze of encouragement.

"Popular house," the clerk said.

"What do you mean?" Sara glanced at Thad, her face scrunched up in confusion.

"Someone else was in last week asking about the same house."

"Do you know who?" Thad asked. Could someone else know about the key? The cops thought the break-in had been random, an easy opportunity, as the house had been empty for weeks. But who could have known about a treasure? He hadn't, and he'd worked on most of the house, from rebuilding the deck to stripping wallpaper and painting rooms. He'd seen no evidence of a secret room or passageway, nor heard the Moffitts mention it.

"No, I'm sorry, I don't. I remember addresses but not people," she said.

"It's okay. It was probably the estate lawyer," Sara said. "Do you have the blueprints?"

"Actually, no, not the original plan. I'm sorry. According to the records, they built the house in the late 1800s. Back then, papers were stored in the courthouse, which went up in flames almost a hundred years ago, destroying everything. I have copies from 1955 when renovations were done. Will that work?"

"Yes, please." Sara paid the fee, and they waited for the clerk to make copies. "I'm excited and nervous. Does that make sense? I mean"—she looked around and dropped her voice to a whisper—"what if Julie was right? What if it shows a you-know-what?"

He leaned closer and whispered, "Then we see if the key will open the door."

Sara laughed and shook her head. "That's a very practical answer."

The clerk returned with rolled-up prints. Sara thanked her, and they stepped out of the office. He spotted an empty table across the hall. "Want to spread the plans out over there?"

"No." She shook her head. "I don't want to take the chance someone might see or hear us. Let's look at them in the truck."

Once inside the cab, Sara didn't immediately unroll the plans. She worried her lip, which he was learning was her tell. She turned to him with the blueprints still clutched in her hands. "Who do you think was asking about these last week?"

"You don't think it was the lawyer?" Thad had his doubts, but he didn't want to fill her head with his fears.

"Why would she have come in? She had all the information she needed from my grandparents. Well, except for my current address, but the town clerk here couldn't have helped with that issue."

"I don't know. You should give her a call and ask." Thad reached for the prints. He suspected that the visitor and the burglar were the same person and that it was her cousin, Billy whatever-his-name-was. There was something off about that guy. His claim to have been close to Royal and Marian this past year didn't add up. Thad had not only done a lot of work for the Moffitts, but after Marian passed away, he stopped in often and visited with Royal. Not once had he ever run into Billy or heard about him. Him showing up right after Sara moved in, right after an interrupted home invasion... For now, he'd keep his suspicions to himself until he had proof. After all, it looked like Billy might be Sara's last remaining family member, and Thad wasn't about to take that away from her without solid evidence.

"I'll call the lawyer when I get home today, but I think it was whoever broke into the house. Someone knows something. I just wish I knew what they were looking for." She let out a deep sigh.

Thad tapped her knee with the blueprints. "We'll figure this out. It was probably the lawyer getting a copy of the deed or something for her record. Hazardville isn't a high-crime area. I know I keep saying that, but it's true. And you heard the cops. Bored teens or some random crook taking advantage of an empty house. Now that they know the house is occupied, they won't be back."

Sara graced him with a smile that lit up her entire face. "I'm sure you're right and I'm just paranoid from watching too many crime shows where the detective says they don't believe in coincidences." She laughed at herself as she pointed to the papers in his hands. "You ready to find out if *X* marks the spot?"

"You bet." He unrolled the papers, giving Sara one end to hold while he took the other end. He ran his finger over the design, following the map of the house from room to room. After several minutes, he rolled it back up and slipped the rubber band around the prints. He shook his head, and they left for the parking lot.

Sara's shoulders slumped as she stared out the truck window. A frown stole the excitement she'd shown a few minutes before. She turned to him as he laid the prints on her lap.

"Well, that's a bummer. I was really hoping Julie might be right and this would lead us to a family treasure. Wouldn't that be something? But, on the bright side, whoever came last week looking for the prints just found an ordinary house." Her voice and smile didn't match. One said disappointment while the other said no big deal.

"Hey, don't give up hope yet. There might still be something to find. We just have to keep looking. After all, if it was on the blueprints, it wouldn't be a secret, right?"

This time when she smiled, it was free and easy. "You're right. I'll just keep looking, and maybe you can help when you have time."

Thad pulled out his phone and typed a quick message to his friend, Lisa, a town librarian and a bit of a history buff. He asked her if she could pull any info on the house for him and let him know when it was ready. Within seconds, he got a reply. He told Sara about the request then started the truck. "I know what will cheer you up." He winked and headed back to Hazardville.

As promised, Thad gave her a driving tour of Hazardville. It took longer than five minutes, but Sara enjoyed every minute. How could she not? Thad was like a living history book. Not to mention his voice. Deep, a little raspy, and soothing. He made her forget all about her earlier disappointment over the blueprints. Sure, it would have been great to find a secret room in her new house, but in truth, there probably wasn't one. The key most likely went to an old grandfather clock or rolltop desk or was a favored knickknack. As for the robbery, she prayed the police were right and that it had been a crime of opportunity.

She put all of that out of her mind as she checked out her new town. What she'd imagined Hazardville to be and its reality were one-eighty of each other. She'd admit, she'd thought all towns in Connecticut looked like Stars Hollow from her favorite TV show growing up. But Hazardville didn't have a cute town center with a pavilion or a funky tiny movie house in someone's basement. It had a river running on the edge of town, with several parks and walking trails. It had some cool old buildings like the Hazardville Institute that looked like a courthouse but had really been a community center. Then there was the redbrick Hazardville Hotel with the white facade and second-floor balcony that looked straight out of a movie set. They had split up most of the building into smaller retail units, like the hair salon that she'd have to check out. Upstairs still had rooms for rent.

Thad shared all of this with her along with stories of growing up in the area. She enjoyed listening to his voice, to the excitement and sometimes disappointment as he talked about home and friends and the changes in the area. The one thing she hadn't expected and was sure she'd miss was the absence of tall evergreens. Come winter, she was going to miss color.

Pretty soon, Thad pulled into the driveway of a local farm. The barn looked like a good wind would send it sailing. She really hoped they didn't house any cows in there.

"What's this?" she asked.

He parked next to a white building with picnic tables and children's play equipment out front. "The best ice cream you'll ever have."

"Have you been spying on me?"

Thad's head twisted around as his brow scrunched down and his mouth hung open like he didn't know what to say at first. "Of course not. Why would you ask that?"

"Ice cream is my weakness. My number-one comfort food. It's better than a warm hug on a chilly night."

Thad laughed as they exited the truck and then took her hand, pulling her toward the building and the menu posted on the side. "Sounds like you haven't been getting hugs from the right people. Although, I will agree, ice cream is up in the top ten of the best foods ever, along with pizza and tacos."

"Well, yeah. Who doesn't like those?" She perused the listings and had to laugh at some of the names. "Do I want to know what flavor 'cowabunga' or 'compost' is?"

"Just be brave and try one without knowing."

"Hmm." Her bravery reserve for the week sat at empty. "I'm going to get a sweet cream sundae with butterscotch syrup and extra whipped cream. Next time I'll go wild and try something else."

Thad placed their orders as she wandered around, checking out the farm. Off to one side was a sign for a pumpkin patch. It would be fun to come back here in the fall and pick pumpkins and go on a hayride while drinking apple cider. Maybe even with her current companion. That was, if she stuck it out and stayed in Connecticut. She still needed to figure out a job and whether or not she was going to keep a house that was way too big for her. And it wasn't just a job she wanted but a career. So far, nothing she'd tried had stuck.

Washington State was big on coffee, tourists, and technology. None of which interested her—except for the coffee, and that was only to drink. She liked people but disliked sales. Pushing people to buy stuff they didn't need wasn't her cup of tea. Sitting behind a desk? She'd tried and had about lost her mind to boredom. She had to be up, moving around. Although she had liked the portion of her job related to social media and creating content for her company.

Maybe she should go back to school? She loved animals. So, maybe become a vet tech? She sent up a silent request for guidance.

"You look about a million miles away." Thad's deep voice swept over her. "Everything okay?"

Sara took the offered sundae with the mile-high whipped cream, and her worries melted away. Ice cream made everything better. "It's perfect. The sun is shining. I'm getting to know my new home with the help of a new friend, and I have this. What could be better?"

They sat at a table as they ate their treats, and Thad shared more of the town's history and events. Next month, in the next town over, was the Four Town Fair.

"You should find your grandmother's zucchini bread recipe and enter it. She used to win every year."

"Is that the one Mrs. Newington enters too?"

"Yep. You can keep the tradition going."

"Or I can let her have a chance to win this year."

"Honestly, I think she likes the challenge. Besides, just because you have your grandmother's recipe doesn't mean you're as good a baker as she was." His playful half smile told her he was joking.

"Or maybe her baking genes were passed down in the family?" Sara shot back.

"I'm happy to taste test anytime you want to try that theory out." Thad reached out, snagged a lock of hair the wind had blown across her face, and tucked it behind her ear. Softly. Gently. With care, making Sara's heart beat a little faster.

"I'll keep that in mind." As she dug into her sundae with the sun warming her face, she discovered that she was over the moon about moving to Hazardville. She had definitely made the right decision.

The conversation flowed easily between the two of them. Not for the first time, Sara felt as if she'd known Thad much longer than just a couple of days. They talked about all the usual subjects people covered when getting to know each other: hobbies, movies, music, likes, dislikes. They both liked action movies and comedies. She loved to bake. He loved to eat. They both liked amusement parks and high-speed roller coasters and disliked rides that spun in circles. And they both valued family and faith.

"I was thinking—" Thad's phone cut him off. "Excuse me, I should take this." He stepped away for a minute as he talked to whoever was on the phone. When he returned, he had his hands shoved in his pockets and his shoulders pulled in.

"Is everything okay?"

"I was going to ask if you'd like to go out to dinner with me tonight, but that was a longtime client with a repair emergency. Let me get you back to your car." He opened the truck door for her, and Sara touched his arm.

"About dinner?"

"Yeah?" His gaze met hers, and she could see a spark of hope.

"How about a rain check for tomorrow?"

"I know the perfect place."

A few minutes later, they were back in front of Hazard Coffee House and Sara's car. She didn't want the day to end. Being with Thad... She couldn't remember the last time she'd felt so light, so carefree or happy.

They set a time for their dinner date, and before she knew it, she was standing alone, watching his taillights disappear. She would have grabbed a coffee to go, but the shop was closed. As she turned to unlock her car door, a man dressed in black with a ski mask over his face jumped out from behind a nearby bush and grabbed her arm.

✑❧ Chapter Five ❧✑

Sara gasped, jerked her arm from his grip, and stumbled against her car, her fingers fumbling for the alarm button on her car key fob.

"Give it to me," the man demanded, holding his hand out.

"You're wasting your time. I've only got about five dollars in cash."

"I don't want your cash. You know what I want," he said.

Okay, talk about weird. What thief turns down cash? Granted, she didn't have a lot of money on her. She took a step to the left. If she could get to the smoothie shop next door, she doubted he'd follow. Not that she valued her purse or the contents more than her life, but replacing her ID, credit cards, and phone would be a huge pain.

"Look, I have nothing of value, but I'm happy to give you what cash I do have."

The thief took a step closer. Sara took another step to the left. He reached out and grabbed the strap of her purse. Then something caught his attention, freezing him in place. Sara looked around quickly. She didn't want to be surprised by a bigger foe.

The door of the house next to the coffee shop opened. A woman's voice called out. *No, Julie,* she cried out silently. Sara didn't want her new friend in danger. She released her hold on her purse. It wasn't worth it.

Instead of yanking the bag off her shoulder, the man released his hold. "What am I doing?" he mumbled. He looked up, his dark brown eyes meeting hers. "I'm so sorry."

The next thing Sara knew, the guy was gone. He ran down the block and around the corner, out of sight. She'd heard people were polite in New England, but a remorseful mugger? That was a new one.

"Sara," Julie called. She had a trash bag in one hand and her cell phone in the other. "Is everything okay?"

Sara collapsed against her car, heart pounding like a war drum. What was going on in this town? She had done research before moving across the country. Everything she read pointed to Hazardville being a safe, quiet place to live. Yet in the two days she'd been here, her house had been robbed, and someone had almost mugged her.

Whoever wrote those reports had a different definition of safe than Sara.

Julie, having reached Sara's side, wrapped her arms around her. "You're shaking like a Chihuahua in a snowstorm. Come on, let's get you inside, and then you can tell me what happened."

Sara let Julie lead her inside the small house, where bright colors exploded before her eyes and the scent of vanilla and strawberries enveloped her in sweetness. Sara sat on a short, plush couch, and a few minutes later, she had a cup of hot tea in her hands and Julie at her side.

"Are you okay? I came outside to dump the trash and saw you standing there and some guy running away. Where's Thad?"

It took a few moments for Sara to find her voice. She didn't want to worry Julie, but her friend was also a single woman and needed to be warned about the crime in her town. "He had a work emergency and dropped me off. Before I could get in my car, someone mugged me. Well, almost mugged. It was so weird."

"Oh wow. Let me call the police." Julie picked up her phone, but Sara stayed her hand.

"Wait. I said *almost* mugged. I thought you and Thad said crime was low here?"

"It is. I mean, sure, stuff happens…some vandalism on abandoned buildings, teens getting into mischief, the occasional B&E or cars broken into, but nothing in broad daylight."

"That's what my research showed as well, but the last couple of days have proven otherwise. Plus, this was odd. I was afraid, but I wasn't. Does that make sense?"

"No, not really." Her friend didn't let go of her phone. "You might be going into shock."

"I offered him the cash I had, but he didn't want money. He even said so."

Julie got up, disappeared into the kitchen off the living room, and came back a moment later with two plates, each topped with strawberry shortcake. "Here, sugar always helps."

Sara took the plate but didn't eat. She was too perplexed for even sweets. "He apologized and then ran off. Although, I think you scared him away, so thank you."

Julie ate a spoonful of whipped cream and berries before saying anything. "Did he say what he wanted?"

"He said I knew what he wanted. But then you opened the door, and he apologized and took off. This has been a strange couple of days. First the break-in, then finding the key and my grandmother's journal.

Someone else visited the public records office just last week asking about my grandparents' house, and now this polite would-be mugger."

Julie grabbed her phone again, fingers flying over the keypad.

"What are you doing?" Sara asked.

"Texting Thad. Plus, we should file a police report. They might not do anything, but they might put on extra patrols or notify neighborhood watch or something. Right?"

"I'm beginning to think this all ties together. Someone knows or thinks my family has a hidden treasure that's worth a lot. But they don't know where it is. That same person tried to get the original blueprints and, like me, found out those are long gone. So they broke into the house, not expecting to find the new occupant. Now that they know I'm here, they've decided I have the answers they're looking for, but the joke's on them."

"How's that?" Julie paused before scooping up more dessert.

"Because I don't have the answers. In fact, I probably know less than they do." A frustrated sigh escaped. She hadn't come to Connecticut to unearth a family secret. She'd just wanted to get to know her grandparents, even if it was secondhand knowledge. Maybe start a new life where she didn't see memories of her parents everywhere she went. Find a job she liked and maybe even someone to share her life with.

She hadn't planned on becoming an amateur sleuth.

Julie slipped an arm around her shoulders and pulled her in for a side hug. "I think you're right. Thad's on his way over, and he agrees we should call and report this. Then I think you should stay here for tonight. See if the police can solve this. You're like a sitting duck alone in that big house."

She knew Julie was trying to comfort her, but telling her she was a target didn't settle her nerves. A soft knock at the front door had Sara juggling her plate like a hot potato.

No, her nerves weren't shot at all.

Thad arrived at his sister's house to find Sara ashen and jittery. She refused the invitation to stay the night with Julie but allowed Thad to follow her home after they filed the police report, to make sure the house was empty and secure. There were no signs of tampering. All the doors and windows were secured, but he didn't feel right leaving her. Too much had happened in a short amount of time.

He told himself he was just going to watch from a block away for an hour or so, but with each passing hour, he found it harder and harder to drive away. What if her would-be mugger was the burglar? What if he came back late into the night when Sara was alone?

He couldn't do it.

So he sat there all night long. He got out of the truck a few times to stretch his legs and take a short walk down the street, looking for anything suspicious. At one point, Mrs. Newington popped her head out the door to give him a look. He nodded, and she went back inside. Since the police didn't show up and roust him out, he figured it was safe to stay.

Just after dawn, movement from an upstairs window caught his attention. Sara had thrown open the curtains and windows. A few minutes later, the front door opened, and she waved to him. Busted.

Thad pulled his truck into the driveway and approached Sara as she stood on the front steps, hands on her hips, looking skyward. He was pretty sure he heard her praying for strength.

"Morning," he called out.

"Thad, what are you doing here? Shouldn't you be home in bed sleeping?" She crossed her arms. As she waited for his response, her toes tapped. Oh boy, he'd seen that exact look on his mom, his sister, and a few of his former teachers. He wouldn't be surprised if little girls learned that stance in kindergarten.

"Would you believe I'm an early riser?" he ventured.

"No." The response was short, clipped, and filled with frustration.

"Confession time. I was worried about you after the last couple of days."

"Did you sleep in your truck last night?" She spun around, storming for the door. "Thad, that's crazy. Were you planning to tackle my assailant if he returned?"

"No. I'm not stupid. I would have called the police and then you so you could lock yourself in your room until they arrived."

She blew out a breath then wrapped her arms around her middle. Tears gleamed in her eyes. "I'm sorry. Sleep evaded me most of the night, and now I'm grouchy. I couldn't shake the feeling someone was watching me." She rolled her eyes and gave a shaky laugh. "If I'd known it was you, maybe I would have slept better. Look, let's start over for the day. Good morning, Thad."

"You look beautiful." Oops. He hadn't meant to say that out loud, but when he saw her reaction, he didn't care. Her cheeks colored. Her hand went to her hair that she'd pulled up into a messy ponytail. Her eyes lit up with pleasure.

"Thank you. Would you like to join me for coffee on the deck?"

He followed her through the house and into the kitchen, noting she'd cleaned this level. She handed him a plate of pastries, and they made their way out the kitchen door. Most of the backyard was still swathed in nighttime shadows, yet where the sky peeked through the trees were streaks of orange, pink, and blue. Birds sang overhead as a couple of squirrels raced from tree to tree.

"Did you spot anything unusual last night?" She took a sip of coffee, closing her eyes as she inhaled deeply.

"No. It was a quiet night, although I'm sure the next time Mrs. Newington sees me, she's going to give me a lecture about stalking."

"Thank you for making sure I was safe, but please don't do that again. First, how are you supposed to function today without sleep? Second, you could have been hurt."

"Sara, your mugger apologized to you. Still, we don't know if he's the same person who broke in here or not. If I were a betting person, my money would be on him being one and the same. He's after something he thinks is in this house. We need to figure out what he's after. Maybe then we can figure out who our villain is."

"That's what was keeping me up all night. I think Julie was on to something with her secret room or passageway, and that key opens the door. Maybe that's where my grandparents hid a chest with all their valuables. Priceless stamps or coins? Those can be worth a lot of money. Or maybe it's jewelry this person is after?"

"I know the blueprints showed nothing out of the ordinary, but you could be right, and the only way we'll know is to start looking."

"But where? This place is huge." Sara glanced back at the house. "I already tried all the interior doors and the desk drawers." Despite her hand shaking as she set her mug on the round, glass-topped table, she flashed him a smile. "Maybe we should look around the yard and garage and see if we can find a giant *X*."

He liked that she'd kept her sense of humor and adventure. He couldn't imagine moving across the country, not knowing anyone, and dealing with what she had for the past couple of days, all while facing that her family was gone. Sara Loomis was not only brave but strong, and when she flashed that playful smile, the rest of the world melted away for him. There were a few things on his calendar for the day that he mentally shifted around. He wanted nothing more than to spend the day with Sara and make her smile.

"I've always found starting at the beginning is best. Let's check out the basement," he said.

"The basement?" Her voice rose an octave. "Please tell me it's not dark, damp, creepy, and filled with spiders."

"Not even close." Thad held out his hand, and Sara laced her fingers with his as he led the way downstairs to a completely finished area with built-in shelves and cabinets. Sara walked around, her fingers trailing along the counters, only to rub them together and shake her head.

"It's not even dusty. It's so organized."

"Like I said, your grandfather was a bit of a neat freak. It doesn't look like whoever broke in came down here."

"Thank goodness. It would take days to put everything back in these boxes. What's in here, anyway?" She pulled a box forward and popped the top to pull out a porcelain angel with lace wings. "This is beautiful."

Thad pointed to the labels on each shelf, noting what was stored there. CHRISTMAS, EASTER, TAX FORMS, SCHOOL RECORDS.

It looked like the Moffitts saved everything. He moved a few boxes to the side and tapped on the wall with his knuckles.

"What are you doing?" Sara put the Christmas tree topper back.

"Here, listen."

Sara moved in close until her shoulders brushed against his as she leaned forward on her tiptoes. He tapped the wall again. "Hear that? Behind the drywall is concrete. All these walls should sound that way."

For the next hour, they made their way around the room, shoving boxes to the side and tapping on the walls. For good measure, Thad did the same with the floor. Honestly, if he was going to add a hidden room, the basement would be a good place do that, since it was all underground. The upper floors would be harder because the different dimensions would be noticeable.

"I think we can safely cross the basement off for having any hidden sections," he said as his gaze scanned around the room. "What if it's not the key they were after? What if, whatever it is, this prize is hidden in plain sight?"

Sara walked over to the shelves labeled MARIAN'S STUFF. "I was thinking the same thing, except it's going to take days to go through all of these boxes." She tugged one from the upper shelf. The box didn't budge at first. Thad reached for it, his arms framing Sara as he grabbed the box. All she had to do was lean back, and they'd be touching. He could wrap his arms around her and hold her like he'd been wanting to do since they left the creamery the day before. He took a beat, breathing in her sweet, tropical scent.

She gave him one of those mischievous smiles before ducking under his arm and out of reach. "Thanks," she whispered, almost shyly.

"I didn't want it to fall on your head." He set the box on the empty counter. "Sara, I—"

Before he could finish, they heard a door close upstairs. Thad told Sara to stay put. He ran up the stairs to find Mrs. Newington in the entryway.

CHAPTER SIX

"Thaddeus." The disdain in the woman's voice raked over Sara's nerves. "I was looking for Sara. Is she here?"

Sara pushed past Thad. "Right here. How can I help you, Mrs. Newington?" She had forgotten to lock the front door. Stupid mistake. Not that she thought her neighbor was behind any of the unpleasant events, but she had to ask. Who walks into someone else's house uninvited?

Mrs. Newington stepped closer and leaned down. She whispered, at a rather loud level, "Are you all right, dear? I saw the police here the other day, and then, late last night, I saw Thaddeus parked on the street."

Sara pasted on her best customer-service smile, the one she'd mastered while working at a children's pizza place in college. "Yes, of course, I'm fine. Thad is just helping me with a project."

"At one in the morning?" Her brow shot up. "I would expect the Moffitts' granddaughter to behave better. And what about the police? Normally, this is a quiet neighborhood."

"Just some mischievous teens. Nothing to worry about."

"Well, you can't blame me for asking." She fingered her gold necklace, gaze darting to Thad and back. "Have you heard about the Four Town Fair next month?"

"I have."

"I suppose you'll be entering your grandmother's recipe in the baking contest?"

"Actually, I don't think I will. I don't even know where or which recipe it is." Sara didn't miss the slight lift of Mrs. Newington's chin or the spark of interest. "Maybe I'll enter something else."

"Well, I could help you look through your grandmother's recipe collection to find it, if you'd like. It really is delicious zucchini bread, and a family recipe like that shouldn't get lost."

"Thank you for the offer." Sara didn't want to be at odds with her neighbor, even if she and Grandmother were rivals. "I'm still in the process of settling in, but once I do, perhaps we can set up a time for recipes and coffee?"

"That sounds lovely." Mrs. Newington glanced at Thad, her brow raised in that questioning way. "Thaddeus."

Once her neighbor left, Sara flipped the dead bolt into place and turned back to Thad. "Is it me, or was that weird?" Sara still didn't think Mrs. Newington was her burglar, but the entire visit had an odd vibe to it.

"No, it isn't just you. What was she doing walking into your house uninvited? We may be a small community, but we're not that cozy."

"Living with locked doors and closed windows makes me feel like a prisoner in my own home. I hate it, and I won't do it." Sara dropped onto the stairs. "Sorry, I didn't mean to snap. The last few days have been stressful. I'm sure Mrs. Newington was just trying to be nice. Maybe she regrets the harsh words she shared with my grandmother and is trying to extend an olive branch to me."

Thad sat down on the step next to her, their shoulders brushing, and laced his fingers with hers. The warmth from his hand filled her up, dissolving the black mood that had formed. In its place she felt better, excited even, about all the right things—learning about her family, making new friends, fresh starts. All the things she'd moved east to find. She wouldn't let a few random events deter her from her new and better life.

"Here's what I propose," she said. "You go home and get some actual sleep, because tonight we have a date." Or maybe not. He had been up all night and might have work to do. Should she postpone? "Or if you'd rather, we can reschedule?"

"No way. I'm a man of my word."

"In that case"—she smiled as she tried to control the silly grin on her face—"go get some sleep. I want to look through some of those boxes in the basement. Maybe I'll find a clue or even the treasure itself."

Thad squeezed her hand before releasing it to stand. Guilt swamped her as she studied the dark circles under his bloodshot eyes. She should have sent him home first thing that morning, not drawn him into her drama of a life.

"Promise you'll keep the door locked? Just for now, until things settle down?" His gaze darted from her to the rear of the house, then to the front, as if he was cataloging all the access points. His concern was sweet and touched Sara.

"Cross my heart." She left off the next line because saying "hope to die" would not set either of them at ease.

He leaned down, brushing a soft kiss on her cheek before letting go of her hand. "I'll see you at six. Does Italian food sound good?"

"Sounds perfect." She closed the door behind him and turned the dead bolt. She made a quick stop in the kitchen for fresh coffee and another scone before returning to the basement. She had a few hours to delve into her grandparents' personal lives and to obsess over that sweet, caring kiss.

The box marked MARIAN'S THINGS turned out to be a time capsule and memory box combined. Sara shifted through old photos—some of her grandparents as newlyweds, some with her mom as a baby, then as a child, and some over the last few years. Someone had written the date and captions on the back of all the pictures. Sara picked out a dozen or so with plans to frame and hang them in the living room. She smiled over saved artwork that her mom brought home from school, noting she must have inherited her lack of an artistic gene from her mother. A rubber band bound a small stack of postcards addressed solely to her grandmother that marked her parents' journey from Connecticut to Washington.

The messages on the cards weren't long or detailed. For the most part they all had the same note: *Love you, miss you! Jessie.*

Tears filled Sara's eyes, blurring her vision. She missed her parents beyond words. The accident that took their lives left a hole in her heart and life, and these postcards made her question her relationship with her mom. She'd thought they were close. Sure, Mom wouldn't talk about her parents, but otherwise, Sara believed they shared everything. Now she knew that wasn't true. Her mom had sent postcards to her parents. She had sent letters with Sara's school pictures. Why hadn't her mom talked about her parents? Why did she keep Sara from them all those years?

Fat chance of finding out now.

Unless.

Unless she could discover a reason in one of her grandmother's journals.

Sara exchanged the box of mementos for another box marked JOURNALS. If she couldn't uncover the mystery behind the key, perhaps she could discover the reason for her family's rift. The box contained a dozen journals. The earliest dated to Grandmother's early twenties and talked about life as a newlywed. Sara had already read the journal that covered her mother's senior year and when she first left. It hadn't provided any answers for her. Maybe this one would. Unfortunately, there was a five-year gap between the two journals. Sara scanned the others. The most recent journal began a year ago, six months before her grandmother's death. She put that on top of the other, carefully boxed up the rest, and returned them to the shelf.

The sun shone overhead while the leaves on the trees danced merrily. Sara grabbed a cool drink and the two journals and headed out to her deck. She should be safe there in broad daylight. For the next several hours, she lost herself in her grandmother's words.

The alarm on her phone sounded. It was time to get ready for her date with Thad. Sara glanced at the journal and then back to the time. She was reluctant to stop reading, but excitement filled her as she thought about the evening ahead.

Thirty minutes later, the doorbell rang, and Sara practically skipped down the stairs. Thad hadn't said where they were going, other than Italian food. Knowing herself and her propensity to spill or drop food, she wore a black blouse with red swirls that formed loose-shaped hearts, a black skirt, and matching sequined flats. On the other side of the door, Thad waved through the frosted-glass window.

She opened the door, and what she saw stole her breath away.

Her handyman was cute and rugged in his work attire of worn jeans, T-shirts, and boots. But this version looked like a man in charge and on a mission.

Black suit, deep burgundy button-down shirt sans the tie, shiny black leather shoes.

Holding a bouquet of white, pink, and red roses.

"You look amazing," he said.

"As do you. Sleep agrees with you." The dark circles and blood-shot eyes of earlier were gone. "Let me put these in water, and then we can go." She headed to the dining room, where she selected a crystal vase, and then bopped into the kitchen. Thad followed.

"How was your afternoon? Discover any new family secrets?"

Sara fluffed the flowers before setting them on the kitchen island, grabbed her purse, and laced her arm around Thad's. "Maybe. Let's wait until dinner to dive into that topic. I missed lunch, and I'm starved."

The drive to the restaurant—Vincenzo's—took less than five minutes. During that time, Thad mentioned other places he thought she'd be interested in. What was nice about Hazardville was, even though it was summer, it wasn't packed with tourists. It wasn't the people she minded, but it was nice not to have to fight traffic or search for parking. Inside the restaurant, Thad waved to the hostess, and she seated them immediately. When Sara raised her eyebrows at him, he grinned. "I might have forgotten to tell you my mom is the manager here."

They took a few moments to look over the menu and discuss the options. She was going to go with baked sausage and cheese manicotti with arrabiata sauce. Thad selected the baked gnocchi, and they ordered calamari and tomato-mozzarella appetizers to share.

"Tell me, what's fun to do nearby? I'm thinking I need to get out of the house and explore my new home state."

Thad sat back and let the waitress deliver their beverages. "Lots, it just depends on what sounds good to you. We could hit the amusement park just over the state line. Or head to the shore and explore Mystic Seaport and Aquarium. We've got beaches. Or we could float down the Farmington River."

She liked that he included himself in the plans. They talked while they ate, avoiding the topic of events from the last few days, and she learned her grandparents had been Thad's first paying customers. They hired him when he was sixteen to paint a room. From there, his business grew and, after graduation, he went full-time. She liked that he knew early on what he wanted to do. She was still trying to figure it out.

As dinner wrapped up, a lovely older woman dressed in a crisp white shirt, black skirt, and shiny black flats approached. Her gaze zeroed in on Thad.

"Hey. I didn't know you were coming in tonight," she said.

Thad smiled before he rose to kiss her on the cheek. "Mom, I'd like you to meet—"

"Jessie?" Her eyes opened wide as her hand flew to her chest. She shook her head, blinked a couple of times, then reached out and took Sara's hand. "I'm sorry. You are the spitting image of an old friend."

"Mom, this is Sara Loomis, Royal and Marian's granddaughter."

"Jessie's daughter. You look so much like your mother. It's a pleasure to meet you."

Sara pulled out an empty chair at the table. "You too. Please join us."

She sat down after a quick glance around the restaurant. "I'm Linda Jackson. Looking at you is like being swept back in time. I heard about your parents. I'm so sorry."

"You and my mom were friends, I take it?"

"She was one of my best friends in high school. Sadly, we lost touch a few years after she moved to Washington. Last time we talked, she was ecstatic because she'd just found out she was pregnant."

Thad stayed quiet, letting the two of them talk, and Sara appreciated he didn't mind that her past had hijacked their date. "Can I ask why you stopped talking?"

Linda took her hand and squeezed. "Life. Thad was a toddler. I was working. We'd had a rough winter—broken pipes and lots of water damage. Your mom was working, and everyday life kept us busy. The next thing I knew, it'd been a few years and the number I had for her had been disconnected."

"And you probably couldn't get the number from my grandparents."

"No. I knew Jessie wrote to her mom from time to time, but I don't think she ever forgave her father."

Both Thad and Sara perked up at that last comment. "Why would she be mad at Royal?" Thad asked.

Linda looked down, and when she looked up, sadness filled her eyes. "I should get back to work and let you two finish your dinner. I'll send over dessert. On the house."

"Wait." Sara touched Linda's arm. "Do you know what caused the rift between my mom and her parents?"

"Are you sure you want to know? There's nothing that can be done now." Worry flittered across her face.

"Yes, please." Maybe she shouldn't know, but not knowing ate at her every day. Maybe whatever had happened was so horrible she shouldn't have moved into the Moffitt house. Maybe it would change the way she felt about her mom. No, that was impossible. She loved her mother, and whatever had happened in the past had nothing to do with her.

"Your grandfather wanted your mom to go to college, but she'd met your dad and fallen in love. She wanted to marry Steve, who was a drummer in a cover band back then. Jessie had a beautiful voice and wanted to sing, not become an accountant or lawyer or something else that had her stuck behind a desk all day. She said her soul would die if she didn't marry Steve and follow her dreams."

"She did have a beautiful voice. She used to sing me to sleep when I was little."

"Royal was convinced she was throwing her life away, that Steve would cheat on her because he was a musician. He didn't want his daughter dependent on anyone, especially a man he was sure would break her heart."

"What happened when my mother refused to do as her father wanted?"

Linda looked away and shook her head. "It was terrible. The two of them argued for days, with Marian in the middle trying to mediate. Then Royal told Jessie that if she married Steve, that was it. He wouldn't acknowledge the marriage or her. She would no longer be welcome in his house. The next day, while he was at work and Marian was out, Jessie left. She and Steve eloped and headed west."

"But surely he forgave her. My mom sent postcards and pictures of me."

"As far as I know, the two of them never spoke again. Marian hid all their correspondence from your grandfather. Royal didn't know that his wife and daughter had stayed in touch until after your mom died."

Her heart sank. "So that's it. Love destroyed my family."

CHAPTER SEVEN

Sara opted to take her dessert to go. Originally, Thad had planned to take her on a walk down by the river, but Sara asked for another rain check. Neither said much on the ride back to her place. He got that she had a lot to process with the information his mom had shared.

When they pulled into the driveway, the motion sensor light Thad had installed came on. It was good to see it was working as it should.

"Let me go in first while you wait here, please. I just want to be sure someone hasn't messed with any of the locks while we were out."

"Okay."

Thad locked the truck with his key fob, making sure the alarm beeped. If someone was lurking around or inside, he hoped they would hear the warning and leave. He could usually hold his own, but if he could avoid running into danger, that would be best. He walked along the front porch, testing the windows and inspecting for any breaks. Then he moved on to the front door. Still locked with no signs of tampering. The lock clicked when he turned the key, and the door swung open on quiet hinges. As he walked through the downstairs, he flipped on lights. All looked good on the main floor. The basement door was locked, so he took the stairs up to the second floor. A quick sweep of the upper levels satisfied him that all was well.

He walked outside and opened Sara's door for her.

"All good?" she asked.

He nodded. Escorting her to the house, he placed his hand at the small of her back and scanned the dark shadows of the yard. Maybe after tonight, if all was quiet, they could relax and consider the threat over. It sounded good, but a gut instinct told him the person who had broken in wouldn't stop until they got what they'd come for.

"Thank you for going out with me tonight. I had a good time," he said.

"So did I."

"Up until my mom." He laughed, trying to lighten things up. She'd been lost in her own thoughts since his mom left the table. "Next time we'll go someplace where no one knows us and we can concentrate on our date."

"I'd like that, although in all fairness, I asked your mom to join us, and I'm relieved to know what happened. But he was wrong."

"Who? Royal?"

"Yeah. My dad didn't break my mom's heart. They gave up the band a few years after they had me. My dad wanted to spend more time as a family, and my mom agreed. They both had wonderful careers, and if she'd needed to, my mom could have supported not just herself, but all three of us. Grandfather should have had more faith in the daughter he raised."

They were leaning on the frame of the open door, and Thad reached out and took Sara's hand. He loved the feel of her soft hand in his. "I can't speak from experience as a parent, but I can't imagine it's easy. Trying to protect those you love but not always getting it right. He made a mistake. One I'm betting he regretted to his last day. I think leaving you this house was their way of apologizing."

"I think you're right." She pushed off the doorframe, smiling with light in her eyes. "Anyway, I can cross that mystery off my list. I'd still love to find out what the key goes to and get more information on the house, but that's a task for another day. Thank you again for everything."

"You're welcome." He bent down and brushed a kiss on her silky cheek. "Call me if you need anything."

"You're going home, right? I better not see your truck parked on the street again, Thad." She laughed and waved to him as he reached the truck, and then, as he watched, she closed and locked the front door. A part of him needed to be nearby and make sure she was okay, but he also knew he needed sleep.

After Thad left, Sara double-checked the locks, turned off the lights on the main floor, and made her way upstairs. She had every intention of drawing a bubble bath and soaking in it while she read her grandmother's journals. As she passed her front-facing window, a movement on the street caught her attention. Thinking Thad was outside, she reached for the French door latch, only halting when she got a better look. It was a man, but not Thad. This person was around the same height but bulkier, wider, with an upper chest made for a defensive lineman. He also had light hair. What was he doing just standing there, looking at her house? It wasn't super late, so it was possible he lived nearby and was out for a walk. But why stop and stare at the house?

She didn't know, but a chill ran through her.

She flipped off all the lights and moved out of his line of sight but where she could still see out the window. A few minutes later, the man left, but she stayed vigil for the next hour, just watching and waiting.

After a restless night of sleep, Sara made it to church as the pastor took to the pulpit. She slipped into the last pew. She had loved church ever since she was a little girl. It was the one place she'd always felt at peace. The minute she walked through the doors, her worries washed away. As the pastor's baritone voice carried through the room, Sara closed her eyes and inhaled slowly while a feeling of light, love, and warmth wrapped around her.

Her mind wandered, mulling over the recent events and her future. Coming to Hazardville had been a gamble. At first, she was certain it was the right move and, despite everything, she was still convinced this was where she belonged. And it had nothing to do with a cute, caring handyman. Thad was like a bonus surprise.

Part of her problem was the same old thing. She needed not only a job but a purpose. Her parents' life insurance and the inheritance from her grandparents meant she wouldn't starve, which was great and all, but she couldn't sit around watching the squirrels play all day. Unfortunately, at the end of the hour, she still hadn't come up with a solution. The pastor welcomed everyone to join him on the lawn for light refreshments. She scooted from her seat only to come up fast when she bumped into a body.

"Were you sleeping in church, Sara Loomis?" Thad leaned in close, his voice a mere whisper, but the deep chuckle that followed vibrated all the way to her toes.

"Absolutely not. I was in deep contemplation over the pastor's words." Well, part of that statement was true.

"Uh-huh." Thad steered her away from the crowd toward a table where his sister and mom set out baked goods. "Did you sleep well last night?"

"I wish."

"You weren't still upset about what my mom told you, were you?"

They'd reached the table. Julie and Linda both greeted her with hugs, and Julie handed her a scone to try. Another new recipe. Sara turned back to Thad. "After you dropped me off, there was this man out on the sidewalk, just staring at the house. It was…" She searched for the right term. "Unsettling."

"You should have called me." She could hear the worry in Thad's voice.

"So we both could lose sleep?" She stepped to the side to let others get to the refreshments table. "There was no point. He stood there for several minutes watching me, and then he walked off. I stayed up for a while, just in case, but he didn't come back. The best way I can describe the whole thing is weird. Like he was measuring me up or something."

"Did you get a good look at him?"

Sara described the guy—tall, big, and blond.

Julie stopped adding pastries to the serving plate. "Did he have any tattoos on his arm?"

"He might have. It was too dark to see much. Why?"

She shrugged. "It sounds like Donald Newington. He just moved home a few months ago. He comes into the coffee shop a lot."

"Why would he be staring at my house?"

"Why did his mother walk into your house uninvited?" Thad asked.

"Good point. Anyway, he didn't come back, and it was a quiet night."

Linda handed her son a plate of food and a cup of coffee. "The Newingtons are a different lot, that's for sure. Sorry, I know I shouldn't say that. I'm surprised they're not here. Then again, ever since Donald got into trouble, his parents have stayed to themselves."

"What kind of trouble?"

"He was in a bar fight." Linda lowered her voice to a hair above a whisper. "He ended up in jail for a while. I don't get it. He was always a good kid. Still is, from what I can see."

She joined Julie behind the table, and Thad nodded to someone over her shoulder. "Speaking of different."

Sara turned to see what he was talking about. Her cousin Billy waved.

"Hi, I was hoping to catch you. It's good to see you here. Isn't Pastor Gary great?"

"Yeah." Although Sara couldn't remember most of what he said.

"I was thinking. I could grab some lunch and come over and help you go through your grandparents' things, and we could get to know each other better." His smile reminded Sara of a reluctant kid in a family photo.

"That's a sweet offer, but I'd rather go through things at my own pace."

"Sure. What about lunch?"

Billy had his fists shoved in his front pockets. His gaze kept darting to Thad, which was strange, because Thad hadn't done or said anything. Every fiber in her being told her not to be alone with her "cousin."

"Maybe another time." She laced her fingers with Thad's. "I've already made plans for today."

"Okay. I should get home to my wife anyway. She's got a terrible cold."

As he walked away, his shoulders were slumped and his head hung low. For a minute, Sara reconsidered her response until she recalled his last comment. "If his wife is that sick, why would he offer to help me instead of going home to take care of her?"

"I don't know," Thad said. "There's something about that guy that doesn't feel right."

A new crowd of people descended on the table. Sara made a mental note to ask her lawyer about Billy Bischoff, then joined Thad to serve coffee. The church had a good turnout, and it looked like most stayed. There were groups of adults catching up and kids running around playing tag while the teens congregated off to the side with their cell phones. Sara smiled as a familiar figure approached them. "Mr. Dawson. It's good to see you again."

"Sara, I was hoping you'd be here." He took a plate of pastries from Julie with a wink. "Looks like you're settling in."

"I am, thanks to the Jacksons."

"And at home? You're getting settled there as well?"

"I am. My grandparents created a home filled with warmth." She stepped out from behind the table, as the crowd had thinned considerably. "You were friends with them for a long time, right?"

"Sure was. I moved here right after college, and they were some of the first folks I met. Sure do miss them."

"I can only imagine how much. By the way, you just missed Billy."

"Who?"

"My cousin, Billy Bischoff."

"Sorry, don't know him."

Things kept getting stranger and stranger. How could a good, long-time friend of her grandparents not have at least heard of her cousin? She really needed to call the lawyer first thing in the morning.

"This may seem like a strange question, but did my grand-parents ever mention a secret room or passageway?"

Mr. Dawson scratched his jaw. "Can't say that they did, but then again, if they had, it wouldn't be a secret, now would it?" He winked, and his chuckle let her know he was teasing. "Why do you ask?"

Sara didn't want to share about the key or her theory that it had something to do with the break-ins. "Just gathering information on the house. I'm thinking of turning it into a B and B. That would be a fun marketing point." The idea had popped into her head a few days ago, but until now she hadn't given it any real consideration.

"A B and B? It's big enough, especially with just you living there. While I can't say that it has any secret rooms, I heard a story a long time ago about the people who owned the house before your family. They were pretty well off once, but then the Great Depression and the war took a toll like they did on so many. There was some story about how they were related to royalty and had a priceless brooch go missing."

"Oh wow. That would be a cool backstory for an inn. Do you know if they still live around here?"

"Well, the folks who sold the house to your grandparents are long gone. I think they still have some family. Couple of brothers that were students of mine. Jake and Kevin Winslow."

He gave her the address and then excused himself. Thad joined her at the bench she'd been sharing with Mr. Dawson.

"Learn anything new?"

"Ever heard about the missing Winslow brooch?"

Thad's reaction surprised her. "Sure, everyone around here has, but it's just an old rumor. There's no proof, and it was like a million years ago. Okay, more like sixty or so. Your grandparents and I talked about it once or twice. They never believed it. That's why I didn't bring it up before. You don't think that has anything to do with what's going on now, do you?"

She wasn't about to rule anything out. "Not sure, but I'm going to go talk to their descendants and find out what they know."

~⌒ Chapter Eight ⌒~

They pulled up in front of a single-story home with faded siding, rotten roof shingles, a broken window held together with tape, and a yard full of weeds. The driveway held one rusted-out car perched on concrete blocks along with a souped-up black pickup. A long way from School Street.

"You didn't have to come with me." Sara eyed the home, not hurrying to get out of his truck.

"Do you believe the police's theory that whoever broke into your home was random?"

She shook her head. "That's why I'm here. You said everyone knows the story of the missing Winslow brooch. Who would know it best? Family."

"How do you want to play this?" He'd rather take her home.

"Let's stick with the B and B story." She pushed the truck door open. Thad moved fast to join her as she walked to the front door. She knocked, waited, and then knocked again. "Maybe they're not home?"

"Or they could be sleeping."

Loud footsteps drew closer. A curtain twitched to the right of the door before it opened. The guy stared at them in stony silence for a few moments.

"Hi—"

"Whatever you're selling, I'm not interested."

"Are you Jake or Kevin Winslow?" Thad put his hand against the door to keep it open.

"Who wants to know?" The guy took a step back. Was he going to bolt? What had they gotten themselves into?

"Hi, I'm Sara Loomis. I'm not here to sell you anything. We're actually looking for some information on a house that used to be in your family. On School Street." She explained she was the new owner and thinking about opening a B and B.

Thad's gaze darted around the room behind the guy. It had old, worn leather couches, scarred tables, and cheap artwork. What it was missing was clutter. It also smelled of lemons. Dawson had told Sara that the Winslow parents had moved away. Maybe not. The guy, who'd introduced himself as Jake, invited them in. Sara sat on the couch, and Thad took the spot next to her.

"Can I get you some water or something? We're out of coffee."

"We're good, thanks," Sara said. "I'll try not to take up too much of your time. I was just hoping you could give us some background information on the house. Did your grandparents own it?"

"Great-great or something. Hang on." He ducked out of the room and returned with another guy. Both were in their twenties, slender build with black hair, but where Jake had dark brown eyes, the other had hazel. They shared cheek structure, facial shape, and identical dents in their chins. There was no mistaking they shared DNA. "This is my brother, Kevin. He's the one into history."

"Hi. So the School Street house, huh? Not much to tell. Our great-great-great-grandparents bought the house from the Black family in

1912. Then in the seventies my grandparents sold it. Before that, our family was one of the wealthiest in town. They used to throw huge parties. I heard the governor even attended dinner there once."

"That's cool. You wouldn't happen to know which governor, would you?" Sara had her phone out, taking notes, and she paused for their answer.

"No, but I think it was shortly after they moved in. That all changed after the Great Depression and then the war. Our family held on to the house, but they had to let the staff go. Our great-great-grandfather was the oldest son. His younger brother died during the war, but our grandfather came home a hero. He inherited the house. From there it went to his son, my grandfather, the last Winslow to own the School Street house."

"They must have sold the house when your dad was young." Thad tried to remember what he'd heard about the missing brooch.

"My dad was three. My grandfather got injured at work. Lost a ton of money, and he couldn't handle stairs. So they sold it."

"I'm sorry. That had to have been hard on him."

"Probably. We didn't know our grandparents very well. It's not exactly the exciting story you're looking for."

Sara's thumbs paused over her phone. Was she going to bring up the brooch? Should he? He got an idea.

Thad ran his hand over his mouth. "Sorry, I have to ask because I grew up here and have heard stories. Was your family really royalty? I mean, they moved to Hazardville. It's not Newport."

Sara shot him a smile, and her eyes lit up with interest. "A house owned by former royals could draw guests to a B and B."

Jake and Kevin exchanged a cautious glance. "Supposedly, our great-however-many-times-grandmother. She was like a niece or cousin to the queen of the Netherlands or something."

"You don't have any documentation, do you?" Sara's voice rose with excitement.

"Nah, just family stories."

"No problem. Any other cool facts or stories you can tell me?"

Kevin's gaze shot to his brother. Jake gave a slight head shake. "That's it, really. It's just an old house our family once owned."

Sara stood, pocketing her phone. "No, what you've told me is fascinating. I appreciate the time."

Back in the truck, Thad caught Jake staring out the front window as they left. "Thoughts?"

"Interesting but not helpful. Although, if I do turn the place into a B and B, I can advertise it was once the home to royals and a war hero and a former governor dined there."

"Are you actually going to open one?"

"I don't know what I'm going to do, but it's an idea. There's certainly enough room." She pulled her phone out again and typed a few quick notes. "I'm kind of surprised they didn't mention the brooch."

"Why didn't you?"

"Because something was up with those two and I didn't want to give them any ideas. Whoever was watching my house last night creeped me out, but he was the wrong build for my would-be mugger. But those two... I mean, they have the right build, and they definitely look like they could make it over a six-foot privacy fence."

Thad drove down to the river and parked the truck. "Is this okay? I thought we could use some fresh air and exercise."

Sara jumped out of the truck and headed toward the water.

He followed her. "We have too many suspects."

"We have suspects?" She picked up a flat rock, sidearmed it, and got three good skips across the river. "I thought we had the opposite problem. I know you don't like Mrs. Newington—and we'll save that story for another day—but we agreed she wouldn't have been able to jump my back fence. Her son could have, but he's not the right build for the mugger. So who does that leave us with? And what is the motive? What are they after? The brooch? If so, why now?"

"Maybe you should be an investigative reporter." He tried his own rock. It sank on the second skip. "You're asking all the right questions. As I see it, you're right about the Newingtons. But we have the Winslow brothers. They weren't sharing everything, and they kept giving each other secretive looks. Then there's Billy—"

Sara's rock plopped into the water as she whipped her attention to Thad. "My cousin?" Why was she surprised to hear Thad list Billy? It made perfect sense. She waited to hear Thad's reasons.

"Your cousin, someone I've never heard of, and neither has Mick Dawson. Don't you find that odd?"

"I do, and I plan to call my lawyer in the morning and ask about him."

"Good, because he fits your physical description of the mugger and looks fit enough to climb a fence. Plus, think about it. If he really is a relative, he might feel he should have been included in the will. Also, if he's from around here, he must have heard stories about the missing brooch."

"You're right. So who else is on your list?"

"The possibility that it could all just be coincidence."

They fell silent for a few minutes as they walked, taking in the beautiful day and surroundings. Sara didn't want to think about break-ins, muggers, or lost priceless jewelry. A kind, caring, funny guy walked next to her. Besides, she wasn't the police. If anything else happened, she'd call them. And she needed to look again to see if the humane society had any dogs to adopt. A big one with a loud bark.

"What do you think of the idea of opening a bed and breakfast? Is it a crazy idea?" When she'd first mentioned her so-called plan, she hadn't given it a lot of thought. It sounded like fun, being her own boss. But she had no idea how to even run a business. Plus, there were risks, such as letting strangers into her home. Strangers who might be looking for a rumored lost artifact.

"Have you ever worked in a hotel before?"

"No. I worked at a kids' themed pizza place." Not really the same thing, but kind of. Both could have demanding clientele.

"Do you know how to cook, and do you enjoy it?"

"Yes and yes. My mom started teaching me before I could even see over the counter. I did work in a restaurant. Sort of. Does fast food count?"

Thad chuckled and draped an arm over her shoulder. "It might, depending on the food."

"Chicken, biscuits, coleslaw, macaroni and cheese, and corn on the cob. The other stuff came to us premade."

"You're making me hungry." His stomach grumbled as if in agreement.

"Why don't you come back to my place, and I'll make us lunch?"

"I'd love to except I promised my mom I'd come over when we finished and fix some stuff around her house. I've been putting it off. If I want to remain on the nice list at Christmas, I better get it done."

"Then how about dinner tomorrow night? I'll make you my specialty dish, and you can judge for yourself if it's good enough for paying guests or not." She didn't really have a specialty, other than mac and cheese. It was made from scratch, but it wasn't earth-shattering.

"Sounds like a plan. I'll bring my world-famous brownies."

She elbowed him in the ribs. "World famous? Like, you've won awards and such? Are you a Michelin star recipient for these brownies?"

"No, but my mom says they're the best she's ever tasted. That's the highest award a baker can get."

"Mm-hmm. And do you have any other testimonials?" She enjoyed teasing Thad. He teased her right back. The earlier unease she'd felt at the church melted away in his company, replaced by not just happiness, but a lightness in her soul. His presence chased the darkness that had invaded when her parents died, and he brought her hope. "So, tell me, Mr. Fabulous Baker, who is your spokesperson?"

"Your grandmother once told me my brownies were better than her zucchini bread."

Sara stopped in her tracks. "In that case, bring on the brownies. If they're that good, we won't let Mrs. Newington know. We wouldn't want her trying to steal your recipe."

CHAPTER NINE

Monday morning Sara took her coffee and headed down to the basement. She spent the next several hours pulling one box after another off the shelves. Some went back to their designated spot, and others she set aside for donating or discarding. No one needed her grandparents' tax records from twenty years ago. She set the box of journals on the stairs to take up to her bedroom. For the last few nights, as she'd read her grandmother's words, a connection had formed.

She'd already found out they both loved to bake, but she also learned they shared a love of history and Agatha Christie mysteries. The coffee thing that some might call an obsession came from her grandfather. Both her grandmother and mom drank tea. She'd also learned that the person who decorated the house for every holiday had been Royal. He'd also passed down his stubbornness, first to his daughter and then to Sara.

She'd gotten halfway through the boxes when the doorbell rang. She climbed the stairs and set the box of journals on the kitchen counter before seeing who was at the door. To her surprise, Thad held up a brown bag and waved.

"Hi. Aren't you supposed to be working?"

"Lunch break. It's in the rulebook that I have to take one every day. Come out and join me."

Sara opened the door wider. "Let's go to the deck so we have some place to sit."

"Why not right here?" One of the things Sara had loved about the house from first sight was the amazing wraparound porch. Another was the turret, and the way the porch mimicked its curves. The perfect place to sit with a glass of iced tea and get lost in a good book. Except that the swing was missing. Or had been.

"When did you put the swing up?" She sat and pushed off with her toes as a gentle breeze washed over her.

Thad settled next to her with the brown bag between them. "About five minutes ago. I used to put it up for your grandparents every year."

His thoughtfulness pulled at her heart. How did she get so lucky to meet such a great person on her first day? She didn't know, but she'd take it.

"Thank you." She smiled. "What's in the bag?"

"Lunch." He pulled out two wrapped sandwiches, a bag of chips, an apple, a banana, and two bottles of iced tea. "I wasn't sure what to get you, so I hope this is okay."

He handed her a sandwich, and she unwrapped it with a smile. "A tuna sub. My favorite."

"A tuna grinder."

"What's a grinder?" She took a bite. Sweet pickles. Green onions. Red pepper? Something added a bit of zip. She'd have to ask, because it was delicious.

"That's what you're eating. A grinder. A sandwich made on a long roll."

"We call them subs in the Pacific Northwest."

"In New England they're grinders. If you go to New York City, you might see them advertised as grinders or heroes. Whereas if you go to Pennsylvania, you'll see them listed as hoagies. Just so you know, because I wouldn't want you to starve."

"I appreciate that. How's work going today?" They talked for a bit about the wheelchair ramp he'd started that morning and how the client's dog kept nuzzling him to play instead of work. He had a packed work schedule, but he asked if on Saturday she'd like to go tubing down the Farmington River. Julie and her boyfriend would be there too. Then he turned the conversation to her.

"Everything quiet here last night?"

"All except for that wheeter-wheeter bird singing outside my window before the sun even peeked over the horizon."

"A what?"

"I don't know what kind of bird it is. It sounds like it's saying wheeter-wheeter. So that's what I call it." His deep chuckle warmed her soul faster than the afternoon sun. In the short time she'd known Thad, his laugh had risen to the top of her favorite sounds list, and she wanted to hear it every day. "Oh, I talked to the lawyer. She wasn't the one who visited the public records office."

"Did you ask her about Billy?"

Sara wrapped up the rest of her grinder, her stomach turning. She hadn't wanted to ask. What if he'd been lying? He said he was family. The only family she had left—but he hadn't provided any proof. While she'd made friends with Julie and Thad, she was alone in Connecticut. The house, the journals—they gave her a connection to her past, but they didn't chase the loneliness away.

Still, she needed answers for her own safety and mental well-being.

"He wasn't mentioned in the will, and she's had no contact with him, which means nothing."

"Except no one your grandparents knew has heard of this guy. What proof do you have he's even who he says he is?"

Good point. How did she prove it without alienating Billy? She didn't have his birth date or his parents' names. All she had was his phone number. "I don't have any. Maybe my grandmother had a family Bible? Or I could simply call him and ask how we're related and go from there." She hoped her initial gut instinct was wrong and that she'd just been spooked from the break-in.

"I'm sorry. You want to believe him, but he's hiding something. I just haven't figured out what his game is. Do you mind if I do some subtle inquiries into him?"

Did Thad plan to stalk Billy on social media? Do an internet search with one of those data companies that tell if a person has a criminal record? She'd hate it if someone did that to her. Then again, she couldn't afford to be careless. If she invited him into her home, she needed to know it was safe to do so.

"That's fine, but please, keep it quiet. I don't want it to get back to him if you're wrong."

"He'll never know. Also, I know we talked about dinner here tonight, but would you rather go out? It's a beautiful day, and there's a festival going on a few towns over. Tonight they have a country band I've heard before. They're great."

Oops. She'd forgotten all about cooking tonight. "Wait. Is this a ploy to get out of making your world-famous brownies?"

"Absolutely not." His jaw clamped down, but the grin followed by the laugh won out. "Okay, I may have forgotten last night to go to the store. In all fairness, the band playing tonight really is excellent, and it's the only night they're in the area."

Sara laughed and leaned into him. "It's okay. I forgot to go to the store too. A festival and concert sound perfect. We both could use a night of fun."

Country music had never been Sara's jam. Her parents' band played rock. She grew up knowing classics from before her time. But after a night of good food, a few old-fashioned games, and lots of dancing, she could call herself a fan. At least of this band. The night gave her hope for the kind of life she'd dreamed of. One filled with fun, friends, and love.

They had just turned onto Hazard Avenue when her phone rang. Julie.

"Where are you?" Julie asked.

"On our way home. Thad took me to the summer music festival. Julie, you should have come with us. So much—"

"You need to get home. There are police cars in front of your house."

"What? Why?"

"No clue. I was out walking, and when I crossed School Street, they went flying by. It's only the police, no fire. That's a good thing."

"We're almost there."

"Let me know what happened. And Sara, if you want, you can come crash at my place for a few days."

"Thanks."

She told Thad what Julie had said, and he took her free hand and gave it a quick squeeze. A few minutes later he parked on the street two doors away from her house. She reached for the door handle, her hand freezing an inch away. An invisible weight pressed on her chest. Red and blue lights flashed over the houses. What could have happened that would bring three police cars to her house?

Thad had come around the car, and he opened her door, his hand held out. "Are you okay?"

"Not really. I'm kind of terrified to find out what happened this time."

"I'll be with you every step of the way."

She clasped his hand as she slid out of the truck and made her way to the house. A police officer stopped them.

"Officer, this is Sara Loomis, and that's her house. Can you tell us what's going on?"

The policeman—Officer Petrowski, according to his name tag—looked down at her, and his gray eyes softened. With heavy salt-and-pepper hair and deep grooves in his forehead and around his eyes, she'd guess him to be in his midfifties. Instead of acting cold or aloof, his voice lowered. "You're the homeowner?"

"Yes, and I'm kind of freaked out right now."

"I've heard you've had a rough week." He walked them over to his car. "Your neighbor reported suspicious activity in your back-yard. Patrols found two men trying to break into the house. We've got them in custody. They tried to say they live here and lost their key."

"I live alone." Sara glanced at Thad. He wrapped his arm around her, tucking her in against his side. His warmth pushed away the cold that had seeped into her. "Do you know who they are?"

Officer Petrowski opened his notebook. "Jake and Kevin Winslow. Brothers. DMV lists a different address. Their story is that they didn't update with DMV when they moved."

"They don't live here, Officer. Their family used to own this house about fifty years ago. After that, it was owned by Royal and Marian Moffitt, Sara's grandparents, who left it to her."

"Yeah, we weren't buying their story either." He nodded toward the driveway where four other officers escorted the brothers—both handcuffed—toward the police cars. Maybe now this nightmare would end.

"Sir." One of the other officers addressed Officer Petrowski, who appeared to be in charge. "We'll take 'em in and book 'em for B&E."

"Hey, we didn't break and enter," Jake said.

"We only tried," Kevin said.

She had to wonder about those two. "What were you after?" she asked.

"The Winslow brooch, duh," Jake said. "It belongs to our family. It doesn't matter if your family bought the house or not. We just wanted our family property."

"So you thought breaking in and stealing it was the way to go?" Thad asked. "If you thought something that belonged to your family was in the house, why didn't you just ask Sara about it when we talked to you?"

"Bro, it's a sapphire-and-diamond brooch that once belonged to the Queen of the Netherlands. Our great-great-great-grandmother smuggled the jewel out when she ran away with our grandfather. It's priceless. Sara wouldn't have given it to us."

Kevin's words rang in her head. The Queen of the Netherlands? Holy cow. She'd been through her grandmother's jewelry box. A sapphire-and-diamond brooch would have stood out.

"Do you know where in the house this item is supposed to be?" she asked.

"No. No one's seen it in over seventy years," Sam said. "But our father said it was hidden in the house."

Seventy years? Why would they even think it was still there? Their how-ever-many-great-grandparents probably sold it or the story was just that—a story. "I hate to break it to you guys, but there's no brooch that matches that description. I've been through my grandparents' things. You just ruined your lives over nothing."

After the police left, Sara sat on the porch swing as Thad checked for any damage. Relief swam through her system. Her muscles sagged, and for a minute she thought about sleeping on the swing. Maybe now she could get some actual sleep. She could leave the windows open and let air flow through the house. She might not jump at every creak and sigh from her old house. She could get on with her life.

Thad sat down beside her.

"The back door has some scratches on it I can easily cover up. Otherwise, the lock held. Thank goodness your neighbor called in time."

"I'm relieved. Maybe I should take them your brownies or a loaf of my grandma's zucchini bread?" She snuggled up next to him to lay her head on his shoulder as he slipped an arm around her.

"Did you find the recipe?"

"No, but now that I know what caused my family rift and I don't have to keep looking over my shoulder, I can search her cookbooks for it. I'm still not going to enter it into the Four Town Fair, but I don't want to lose that piece of my family history."

"Family treasures are good, but so is moving forward." He chuckled, and Sara felt his chest vibrate under her hand. "If you can't find it, make up your own recipe. And remember, I'm always happy to taste test."

CHAPTER TEN

For the first time since arriving in Hazardville, Sara slept with the windows open. Even the wheeter-wheeter bird with his five a.m. concerto didn't bother her. She simply smiled and rolled over to go back to sleep. Hours later, after getting dressed, she bounced down the stairs and walked to the Hazard Coffee House. She filled Julie in on the previous night's activity and then ordered a large coffee with extra French vanilla creamer and an assortment of pastries to go. As she approached her house, Mrs. Newington waved from where she watered her flowers.

Sara invited her over for coffee. The two settled on the deck with Sara's grandmother's recipe box in front of her. Mrs. Newington had brought her own. They spent the next hour eating scones and swapping recipes until Sara pulled out a card with worn edges and batter stains.

"My grandmother's zucchini bread recipe."

Mrs. Newington's eyes lit up. "May I? I won't copy it. I just want to see what was so different. Her bread truly was the better one every time."

Sara held the card off to the side where Mrs. Newington couldn't read it. Should she? Would that be breaking her grandmother's trust? While she wanted to get along with her neighbor, she couldn't do it. "How about I read the ingredients but not the amounts? I think, or rather hope, my grandmother would be okay with that."

Mrs. Newington agreed, and Sara listed off what her grand-mother used.

"Aw, so that's it—the pineapple. It made the bread moist and yet not overly sweet." She smiled and set her cup down. "Please say you'll make a batch and at least share a loaf with me. Your grand-mother was a talented baker. I know we had a not-always friendly competition going on, but I respected her ability in the kitchen."

"I'd be happy to bring over a couple of loaves. Then you can freeze some for later to enjoy. Will you enter your zucchini bread in the contest this year?" Sara handed Mrs. Newington back her recipe for a summer salad.

"Actually, I'm thinking I'll try something new this year. I just haven't figured out what yet. Maybe a banana bread or frosted pump-kin cookies." She handed Sara another card. "Don't make this yet. Beef stroganoff is a hearty dish. Save it for when fall comes around."

Sara thanked her and set the card aside to copy later. Now that the police had nabbed the culprits breaking into her house, she could enjoy sitting on the deck with a neighbor. She hadn't given up on finding what the key fit, but for now she wasn't worried about it. Later, she planned to finish going through the basement and then call to schedule delivery of her belongings in storage. Despite the crazy first week, she'd found home.

Mrs. Newington said her goodbye, and Sara got to work on the house. Once the basement was done, she needed to box up clothes and shoes to donate to a nearby shelter. Maybe she'd rearrange the bedroom to make the room her own or buy new bedding. She didn't plan to make any major changes, just small things here and there to add her stamp to the family home.

When she got up to her room, she opened all the windows to let the breeze in. She was taping up boxes when her phone buzzed with a text message.

Billy.

Hi Sara. To answer your question about how we're related. I don't know if it's second cousins or third twice removed. That stuff's confusing. Our grandmothers shared grandparents. Three greats back. I'm betting your gram had a family bible like mine. Look for James and Sarah Harrington, then follow Lydia to Marian for your side. For me, it's James and Sarah to Joseph to Elizabeth Harrington Bischoff (my grandmother). Let's get together soon.

She went to the nightstand to pull out the Bible in the top drawer. At the front was a family tree. It listed the relationships Billy mentioned. She held the closed book to her heart as a heavy weight lifted. She breathed in a deep, calm breath. Tension she hadn't even known she'd held on to disappeared. Life could finally get on. A quick glance at the time told her she better get moving if she planned to rearrange her room and get to the store and back to make Thad dinner.

Before she could get started, the doorbell rang, startling her. She ran down the stairs, hoping Thad was surprising her with lunch again. Instead, a strange man holding a suitcase stood on the porch.

"Can I help you?" Could he be another newfound relative?

"Hi. Nutmegger Security. Thad Jackson scheduled a security system installation. Are you Sara?"

In all the chaos from last night and the relief this morning, she'd completely forgotten about the appointment. Although, did she need a security system now? It might be a waste, and chances were high she'd forget to turn it on half the time anyway, but she knew Thad would feel better with it in place. From what she'd heard, everyone local knew about the missing brooch. When the story of the arrest came out, and what the Winslow brothers were after, who knew what would happen?

"I didn't know there were castles in Connecticut." Sara walked along the stone porch, trailing her hand along the balcony.

"There are others. Saint Clements holds events. Others like Castle Craig and Sleeping Giant are more like observation towers. There's one up in Woodstock that's been in the news a few times. Some guy built a gothic-style castle for his daughters."

"I hope they've got a big family, because I can attest that living in a large home by yourself is not always as fabulous as it sounds." She leaned against a rock column where they could see the state park.

Was she thinking of selling the place? He wouldn't blame her after the past week, but the Winslow brothers were in jail now. "Did something else happen?"

"No. I mean, the house is wonderful, and I'm loving getting to know bits and pieces about my grandparents by living in their home and reading my grandmother's journals. There are other perks like no line for the bathroom and I can watch whatever I want on TV. No one can fuss at me for eating ice cream late in the day, because I'm in charge of the kitchen."

"Sounds pretty great."

"But it can also feel isolating. I still jump at odd noises. I keep thinking, what if someone sneaks in while I'm upstairs? They could hide in the basement or get up to the third floor, hide out, and rob me while I sleep."

She shivered in the afternoon sun as he wrapped his arms around her. If he could, he'd turn the clock back a week and catch those two birdbrains in the act before she ever got to Hazardville. Then she'd feel safe in her home. "You're safe now. Between the door alarms and the security system, no one can sneak in without you and the police knowing. We can have the security company add my phone number as an additional notification. If the alarm goes off, I can be there in minutes."

He'd do whatever it took to make her feel secure, even if it meant sleeping in his truck every night.

"I'll be fine in a couple of weeks. Adding your number to the list would make me feel better." She gave him a tight hug and then stepped away. "Let's go explore. I've never been in a castle before. Out here it looks almost like ruins, but not quite. Like the place is one season away from being abandoned."

He laughed. "Wait until you see inside. It's anything but. The guy who built it, William Gillette, was an actor and known for his love of mystery and drama. Did you know he played Sherlock Holmes on stage?"

"Ah, now the sign out front makes sense."

Thad's first trip to the castle had been in school, maybe fourth or fifth grade. When he saw the sign with Sherlock Holmes and a picture of a detective, he thought William Gillette was the real

Holmes. Since then he'd been here numerous times, mostly to hike the trails through the state park.

They made their way inside, and Sara stopped, causing him to run into her. "Sorry." She moved over. "It's so open. Spacious and cozy, but it reminds me of a rustic inn, not a home. It needs a rug in front of the fireplace and a comfy couch, not that weird little table."

"Anything else?" He got a kick out of hearing the changes she'd make.

"I love that lounge in the corner. Talk about a perfect reading spot. I would get rid of the half-circular couch thing, though, and replace it with a couple of overstuffed chairs, a good reading light, and a small table to hold a drink and snacks."

He'd never thought about the decor before, but she was right. The placement of furniture made little sense. The place didn't feel like a home. "You should become an interior decorator."

"Thanks. It's an idea." They headed upstairs to finish the tour.

Afterward, they headed outside and down a trail. "Have you thought about redecorating your house?"

"Maybe little things. A touch here or there. It doesn't feel right changing up a lot of stuff. Like, who am I to come in there and toss their stuff out?"

"Their granddaughter and the new owner." He took her hand and helped her over a fallen log. "I don't think they intended for you to keep everything the same. They'd want you to make it your home, Sara."

"Okay, there is one thing I'd love to do."

"What's that?"

"Paint. Every wall is white. I was thinking a soft blueish-gray would really soften up some rooms. You wouldn't know a good handyman who can paint, would you?"

"I just might." He pulled her off the path to stand under the shade of a maple tree. If she was making changes, it meant she was staying. The last week hadn't scared her off. He didn't even know how to describe what he felt. Relieved, sure. But it went beyond that. In a short time she'd become an integral part of his life. He didn't want to go a day without seeing her.

The very idea sent his heart skittering. His breathing turned shallow and fast.

"Hey, are you okay?" She laid her hand on his chest. "Do you need to take a break?"

"No, I just need you, Sara." She tilted her head, a small smile lifting her lips. He leaned forward and kissed her. Her hand slid to the back of his neck. If he thought that would slow his heart rate down, he'd been dead wrong. Now he knew—he needed to kiss Sara Loomis every day for the rest of his life as much as he needed to breathe.

When he broke off the kiss, he rested his forehead against hers.

"Wow," she whispered.

"I've wanted to kiss you for days." He placed a soft kiss on her nose. "We should get going. They're going to close soon."

On the way home they stopped and picked up a pizza. After being outside all day, both just wanted something easy for dinner and to relax and watch a movie. Thad didn't really care what they did as long as he was with Sara. The day had been perfect, and he wasn't ready for it to end.

He pulled into Sara's driveway and parked his truck next to her car. He grabbed the pizza box and was making his way around when he heard her yell.

"What?" He hustled to her only to stop at the broken glass on the ground. She was standing in the middle of the mess, tears streaming down her cheeks.

"I'm so tired of being a target."

⸙ CHAPTER ELEVEN ⸙

Sara hadn't left her house in days. If she had it her way, she'd still be there. With the security system on. Behind locked doors. Jumping at every noise. But Thad had other ideas, insisting that she get out of the house, even for a few minutes. She couldn't agree less, but here they were.

"Thad, couldn't you have grabbed groceries for me? Or we could have had them delivered." Good grief, even she could hear that she needed a little cheese to go with her whine.

"Sara, you haven't left the house in a couple of days. You can't let this person control your life."

"Easy for you to say. You're not his target. Let's just get what we need and get out of here. I'm pretty sure I'm breaking out in hives."

He took her hand and steered her toward the produce section. She appreciated what he was attempting to do, but not knowing what she was going to come home and find this time had her freaking out. Not for the first time, she sent up a quiet prayer asking that this ordeal be over.

"We'll be quick."

Thad was true to his promise, power shopping for everything they needed for an all-day picnic. At ten a.m. the temperatures had soared into the nineties and promised to keep climbing. She could have ordered a gallon or two of ice cream and been fine.

In the freezer section, they spotted Mick Dawson. How he could stand to be in a long-sleeved shirt, she didn't know.

"Mr. Dawson, it's good to see you." Thad shook the man's hand. "How are you doing in this heat? I know those window AC units you had were on their last leg last summer."

"Fine. The house is a cool sixty degrees. I installed a couple of those ductless units. Not only are they quiet, but they keep the house like an icebox."

"We may come visit," Sara said. If only she wasn't kidding. She'd have to look into the system he installed, because the old units at her place weren't doing the job. She glanced at his basket and the contents. She didn't know Mr. Dawson was married. "Those are pretty flowers."

"Thanks. They're for my mom, who lives with me. She's been sick, and it's taken a toll on her mood. I'm hoping they'll cheer her up some. She's the reason I have to keep the house so cold. She's got an unusual condition that causes her to overheat quickly and without her noticing."

"Maybe after this heat wave passes, you and your mom can come over for dinner or brunch one day. I'd love to hear your stories about my grandparents."

"That sounds nice." He reached for a container of ice cream, careful not to squish the flowers. "What are you kids up to today?"

"A picnic. I wanted to take Sara tubing down the Farmington River, but they were booked solid already."

"Well, a picnic sounds like a great idea. I'll see you both on Sunday." He waved and left them to finish their shopping.

On the way to the registers, they passed a familiar face in the first-aid aisle.

"Billy." Sara stared at the large bandage on his arm. "Are you okay?"

"Yeah." He held up his arm. "Rosebush attacked me doing yard work. I think it's infected now."

"You should have a doctor look at it."

"Got it covered right here." He pointed to the antibiotic cream in his cart, along with cold medicine. "Do you have any plans for the Fourth? If not, I'd like to have you over for a barbecue at my place."

She glanced at Thad. They hadn't talked about the upcoming holiday, but it was still a few weeks away.

"You're welcome to come too." Billy looked at Thad, although the downward turn of his mouth didn't convey the same message.

Thad shrugged, and she assumed he meant yes. "Sounds great. Let me know what I can bring."

"Sure. I wish we could have you over soon, but Deb hasn't kicked her cold yet, and I'll be in New York most of the time for work."

"No worries. I understand, and I'm just excited to get to know you and your family. You have two kids, right?"

"Yep. A boy, five, and a girl, six. They're a handful, but we love it."

Thad kept quiet while the two of them chatted, but Sara hadn't missed the look on his face. She should have waited to respond to Billy's invitation until after she'd talked with Thad. If he wanted to back out, she'd understand.

She wrapped up the conversation, aware they'd been away from the house longer than she'd intended. Who knew how many people had tried to break in while they were away? Okay, she was being paranoid. She'd turned the security system on. If anyone tried to get into the house, a notification would have pinged her phone. Thad kept quiet as they checked out and then climbed into his truck.

"Why don't you like my cousin?"

"He's a liar."

"What is he lying about? I checked the family Bible. There's a William Bischoff on the family tree."

"I know that's his real name." Thad scowled as he navigated the drive to her house. "But his employer fired him months ago."

"How do you know that?"

"I told you I was going to look into him. His wife, his neighbors, all think he's still working. You know where he goes during the day when they think he's at his job?"

She closed her eyes and sighed. Maybe moving to Hazardville wasn't the right choice. "Where?"

"To the casino. And he's a lousy blackjack player. I wouldn't be surprised if he wasn't the one who trashed your house. Plus, I'm not buying that he got scratched by a rosebush. I drove over to where he lives in Enfield. I saw his wife out in the yard yesterday. They don't have any roses."

"Maybe he got the scratch from another rosebush?"

"Like the one in your backyard where the intruder jumped the fence?"

Cry or scream? Both seemed like good options. She didn't want to fight with Thad. He'd only done what he told her he was going to do, what he'd gotten her permission to do, and then relayed the info. "Can we table the talk of intruders for the day? I appreciate you telling me the truth. I just need a break. I'll find an excuse to cancel on the Fourth."

When they got to the house, Thad hugged her and kissed her forehead. "I'm sorry."

"It's all good. Let's get these groceries inside before the ice cream—and I—turn into a puddle on the driveway."

They set the bags on the kitchen counter. As she pulled out the food, Thad ran back to his truck for the last bag. Sara realized when she set the steaks on the counter that they'd forgotten to get propane for the grill. She went to tell Thad, but he was at the end of her driveway half-hidden by the bushes.

She stepped out onto the front porch. "Thad? Is everything okay?"

He glanced over his shoulder at her then toward the street and whoever was behind the bush. A few seconds later, he returned to the truck, where he grabbed the last bag then slammed the door.

She put her hand on his shoulder. "Hey, what's wrong? Was Mrs. Newington giving you a hard time again?"

"No. Let's get this stuff inside." He stormed off without saying another word.

What did she miss?

Sara followed him to the kitchen. "Thad, who were you talking to?"

"No one important."

"You're clearly upset. Talk to me."

"I can't."

So many secrets. Her parents. Her grandparents. Her cousin, and now Thad. She was tired and frustrated at the situation, at people not being what they presented, of living her life in fear. Thad was the one person she thought she could trust.

"Can't or won't?"

"The person asked me to keep our conversation private."

"I haven't left the house in days. I haven't slept, because the floorboards keep creaking. Last night, I thought I heard someone jiggle a door handle, but I forgot to flip on the motion sensor lights, so I couldn't see who it was. I don't know if it was real or my imagination, but my instincts are telling me someone is watching my house."

He reached for her, but she stepped back, arms wrapped around her middle. If he touched her, she'd burst into tears. She shook her head, refusing to meet his eyes.

"Sara, I promised I'd keep the conversation confidential for now."

"Is that person's secret worth more than my safety? Than my peace of mind?"

"Maybe you should stay with Julie for a few days, give the cops a chance to catch this person without you being in danger."

She'd worry every second. And how long was she supposed to stay away? A day, two, a week, a month? It had been over a week, since they'd made an arrest. But lucky her, there was still someone else out there dying to get into her house.

"You know what, Thad?" When he stepped closer, she pressed against the kitchen counter. "Just forget it. All of it. I can't deal with this anymore, and I don't have the energy for a picnic or stargazing. I need some space."

She needed some time alone with her thoughts, her feelings, and most of all her doubts. She needed some time to pray for strength and guidance.

Thad took another step toward her then dropped his hand. "If you change your mind, call me. I'm not giving up on us."

Thad slammed the back door shut, making the dishes on the shelves rattle. Whatever. If they broke, he'd replace them. Who knew one conversation had the potential to destroy so much—relationships, lives, trust.

He took a moment to gather his thoughts, and as he breathed in deeply, he asked for patience.

Julie popped into the kitchen, a scowl pulling at her features. "I've been trying to call you. We need... What's wrong?" She leaned against the doorframe where she could monitor the front of the store and him at the same time.

"Other than Sara's mad at me?" He'd love to share his burden with his sister, but putting this knowledge on her shoulders wasn't fair either. "It's these break-ins. I'm worried about the toll it's taking on Sara."

"You really like her, don't you?" A slow smile lifted the corners of her lips. Julie pushed off the wall to wrap her arms around him. "I'm glad. Mom and I both like her."

"Don't get your hopes up. I think I really blew it yesterday."

Julie patted him on the shoulder and headed toward the front. "Don't be ridiculous. I've seen how she looks when she says your name."

"Did you talk to her today?"

Julie stopped. "No, she hasn't been in today. Want me to call her? Just to check in, one friend to another?" His sister already had her cell phone out, punching buttons. A few moments later, she tucked it back into her apron pocket. "Maybe she's taking a nap or doing yardwork."

"Thanks for trying."

"Don't give up hope, big bro. Whatever you two fought about, she'll come around and forgive you. You're very hard to keep a grudge against. I should know. I've tried multiple times over the years. Like that time you ate my chocolate Easter bunny."

"How many times do I have to tell you? It was an accident. I thought it was mine."

"In my pink and yellow basket? In my room?" She smiled. "But don't worry, I forgave you a long time ago."

As his sister sailed into the front to help a customer, Thad chuckled. Sure she did. That's why she still remembered after twenty years. If his sister couldn't forget one minor transgression, how was he supposed to have faith that Sara would forgive him for yesterday?

"Hey, Sara's here and asking for you." Julie stepped out of the way so he could pass through the doorway. "I'll give you guys some privacy. Just holler if anyone else comes in."

He gave his sister a kiss on the cheek in thanks. Sara sat at the table in the corner where he'd been sitting the first time he'd seen her. Her gaze was on something out the front window as she picked at her nail polish.

"I stopped by your house earlier." For the first time since they'd met, nerves tangled up his tongue.

"Sorry, I had some errands to run."

"Good." Brilliant conversation. *Just tell her you're sorry already.* "Sara, I—"

"Wait." She held up both hands, making eye contact. "Let me get this out. I wasn't at the house, because I was at a real estate office. I'm putting the house up for sale and going home to Washington."

What?

"No, you can't leave." Julie ran out of the back room, over to Sara, and took her hands. "It's been a crazy welcome, but it'll get better. And you just got here, and we became friends, and I'll…" She sniffed. "I'll miss you."

Sara hugged her. "I'll miss you too. Meeting you and your family was the best part of coming here. But it's all been too much, and look at it this way, you have an excuse to come to Seattle…to see me." Sara's eyes met his over his sister's shoulder. Tears glistened but didn't fall.

"We'll talk, okay?" Julie said to Sara. "I've got some stuff in the oven."

Thad reached out and laced his fingers with Sara's. Something so natural, he didn't even think about it at first. "Can we talk about this?"

"Are you going to tell me something I don't know?" She pulled away. As she crossed her arms around her middle, an invisible wall pushed against him, shoving him further and further away until he was afraid he'd never reach her again.

He refused to give up.

"How about I don't want you to go? And I'm sorry about yesterday."

"It doesn't matter now. Thad, I didn't sign up for all this drama. I came to learn about my grandparents, and I did. Someone doesn't want me here, and they've won because I can't keep living my life looking over my shoulder."

"Sara—"

"No. Don't placate me. Do you know I couldn't sleep again last night? Every time I closed my eyes, I heard weird noises."

"You're just going to walk away from us?"

"Thad, I appreciate you gave your word to whoever, but I can't stay where I can't trust people."

"I understand. I should have told Donald Newington that you needed to know what he shared with me."

"Donald Newington? Why are you telling me now?" She plopped down in the chair. Her stare drilled him to the spot.

"Because I went over this morning to get more information from him and to get his permission to tell you about our conversation." Thad sat across from her. He wiped his palms across his thighs. "First, he stopped me because he wanted to know if I was hiring. He's been looking for a job, but because of his past, he's been having trouble finding work."

"Poor guy. He needs someone to give him a second chance."

Thad understood the guy's frustration. "People are leery of what they don't understand. The other thing he told me had to do with you. He saw someone hanging around your place."

Sara leaned forward and grabbed his hands. "Did he know who it was?"

"No, but I think I do."

"Thad, we need to call the police or confront this person. Is he or she dangerous?"

He thought for a moment. "I don't think so, but I want to hold off on calling the police. I think I know how we can catch him in the act. Can you trust me?"

Sara pulled back, but she didn't let go. "Why?"

"If I'm wrong, if Donald was wrong, we could ruin an innocent life. I want to make sure before I do something that I can't undo."

She nodded as she worried her bottom lip. "How do you propose we catch a thief?"

CHAPTER TWELVE

Under the cover of night, Sara and Thad slipped behind the garden shed in her backyard. They wore jeans, dark shirts, and sneakers. If anyone saw them walking from where he'd parked two streets over, they would look sketchy as all get-out. But this way they blended with the shadows in her yard.

"What if this doesn't work?" she whispered.

"It will. I'm pretty sure our burglar has been keeping tabs on us. If he didn't hear our exchange in the coffeehouse, he'll hear it from Mrs. Newington. She was out watering her lawn when I got here. She loves to gossip, and she was heading out soon, so I'm sure whoever she runs into will hear we had plans for tonight."

Earlier that morning, Sara had gone to Hazard Coffee House during their rush hour. Thad had made a point of asking her out in front of everyone, and not quietly. If he was right, and the person trying to get into her house had been watching them, tonight would be the perfect time to strike again.

Time slipped by. Sara's feet hurt, and her legs cramped from squatting for so long. Had they been too obvious? Or had the person given up? Or maybe he was busy in New York for work? Thad hadn't shared who his suspect was, but she knew he hadn't liked Billy from the start. She still didn't want to believe her cousin was behind it all, but she had to admit, he had motive. Thad had confirmed with

Billy's employer that they had fired him a couple of months ago. Thad had also followed her cousin to the nearby casino and watched him lose at poker then hit up a quick-loan place.

If only he had come to her and asked for help. She wasn't Rockefeller, but she would have done what she could.

"Thad." She tugged on his shirtsleeve then leaned forward to whisper in his ear. "I don't think it's going to happen tonight." As the last words left her mouth, she froze. A dark shape walked through her yard and crept up the back stairs to the door. He was dressed head-to-toe in black, complete with stocking cap. She got her phone out, set it to night sight, zoomed in, and took a picture. Once he opened the door or window, the alarm would go off and the police would be notified. She wanted to have some kind of proof in case he got away.

The man reached for the door then glanced over his shoulder, hesitating.

Had he heard the camera click?

She took another picture. When she zoomed in on the man's face, she gasped.

Thad stepped forward and broke their cover, but the thief didn't run. He dropped into one of the deck chairs and buried his face in his hands.

She could hear Mick Dawson trying to stifle his sobs.

Thad and Sara approached the deck cautiously. Thad had known the man all his life, but he wasn't taking any chances, and Sara appreciated that he put their safety first. When they reached the stairs, another figure turned the corner of the house. Billy.

What on earth was going on? Had the two of them been working together all this time?

"You have ten seconds before I call 911. One of you had better talk." Anger laced Thad's voice.

Billy looked between them and the man crying on her deck. "I was stopping by to drop something off for Sara, but then I saw someone sneaking around the side of the house. I parked my car and came to investigate."

"I see empty hands. What are you dropping off, Bischoff?" Thad's finger hovered over the call button on his phone.

"Pastries from Arthur Avenue in New York. I stopped there on my way home and grabbed some for Deb. I also got some for Sara, since she's new to the area. There's nothing like Arthur Avenue's Italian pastries." He pointed his thumb over his shoulder. "I left them in the car until I knew what was going on."

"Did you know Sara wasn't supposed to be here tonight?"

Billy held his hands up. "No. We haven't talked since I saw you guys at the grocery store. I dropped the cold meds off to my wife and left that afternoon for a job interview."

"That was two days ago."

"Look, Jackson, I'm tired. It's been a long week. I spent all day yesterday in interviews and half of today onboarding for a new job. It took over four hours to get out of New York, and then there was tons of traffic on the Merritt Parkway. I just want to make sure my cousin is okay, give her a welcome gift, and go home to my wife."

Thad bristled. "You've been lying to everyone in your life for months. Why should we believe you now?"

"Leave the guy alone." Mr. Dawson wiped his eyes and slumped even farther into the chair. "Billy had nothing to do with this mess. It was me. I was after the missing Winslow brooch."

He waved everyone off before they could speak. "I've heard about that brooch since I moved here decades ago. I figured it was a fairy tale. A story the ladies came up with to liven things up in our sleepy little town."

"What changed your mind?" Sara sat down in the chair across from Mr. Dawson, no longer afraid. She simply wanted the truth.

"About a month before your grandfather passed, he made a comment. I don't remember it exactly, but something about how he buried the secrets and treasures of this old house after Marian passed. Thought little of it then. Ramblings of an old man in the throes of grief."

"What changed your mind?"

"Desperation." He pulled a napkin with the Hazard Coffee House logo on it out of his pocket and blew his nose. "I might have mentioned my mother is sick?"

"You said she couldn't take the heat." Sara looked to Thad for confirmation. At his nod, she turned back to Mr. Dawson.

"It's more. She's dying. They ran a million tests. Tried I don't know how many medications, and nothing is helping. The medical bills are piling up. The co-pays have drained her savings and mine. At this rate, I won't be able to pay her final expenses."

"A priceless piece of jewelry, stolen over a century ago from the Queen of the Netherlands, would take care of all that and more," Thad said.

"I planned to repay our savings, pay for her needs, and then donate the rest to charity. I'm not a greedy jerk, I promise."

"You knew my grandparents had lost track of me and the house was empty. That was your chance to find the jewel."

"But you moved here. Then I saw you show Julie and Thad a key at the coffee shop, and I figured that held the answer."

"You tried to mug me."

"I apologize again for that. It was wrong of me to scare you like I did. I will regret my actions until I take my last breath."

Tears slipped down his cheeks, and Sara's heart broke for the man sitting across from her. She didn't know what she would have done in his shoes. Hopefully not cross any illegal or immoral lines, but love could make people do crazy things.

Like cut your own daughter out of your life.

"I had given up until you asked me about a secret room."

"Do you know where it is, or were you planning to randomly punch holes in my walls until you found something or ran out of space?"

Mr. Dawson looked away.

"What's this about a secret room?" Billy asked.

"My grandmother mentioned in her journal that my mom spent a lot of time in her secret room as a teenager. I thought maybe the house had a hidden room or passageway and there might be some family treasure locked away."

Billy rubbed his hands over his eyes. "I don't know about that. Your mom had an alcove off her bedroom where the turret is. It was her private space. I remember playing there with her once when I was a kid. She had a curtain over the entrance and said only those she invited were welcome. I can show you."

Sara unlocked the kitchen door then slipped inside to disarm the security system. From there Billy took the lead, up the back stairs to the third floor. Thad followed, putting Mr. Dawson in between them. Billy led them to the bedroom at the front of the house. The room had three windows that overlooked the front yard and three solid walls. It didn't even have a closet.

"Where's the alcove?" Sara turned back to Billy. Fear snaked its way through her. Had he lied? Letting him into the house and following him to the top floor screamed *stupid*. As Mr. Dawson said, desperation made people do crazy things.

Billy walked over to the front corner. He scratched his chin. "I'm sure this was the room. It's been a long time. Maybe it was the floor below. But honestly, I'm sure it was this room and that this corner here opened up into a round tower room. Jessie loved it. There were no windows, so she strung up fairy lights, filled it with pillows, and read in there all the time."

"Thad, did you do any work in here? Wall it up?" she asked.

"Not me. This is probably the one room I've never been in before." Thad ran his hand up and down the wall, then tapped on it. He tapped a little trail all around. There was a depth to the knock one time, and a hollowness the next. He switched back to run his palm from the ceiling to the floor. "Right here, under the wallpaper, is a slight seam."

"Tear the wallpaper off."

Thad glanced at her, brows raised.

"I've never been a big wallpaper fan."

Thad pulled a multiuse tool from his pocket. It took him just a few minutes to catch the edge of the paper and tear a long strip off to reveal a door with a keyhole but no knob.

"Hang on." Sara ran down the stairs to her bedroom and grabbed the skeleton key. She ran back up the stairs, her lungs heaving from the exertion, and she promised herself she'd up her cardio game starting tomorrow. For now, she needed to see what was behind door number one.

Everyone stepped back as she inserted the key, and the lock clicked. A sliver of black space appeared between the wall and door. She wedged her fingers in and slid the door open.

"It's a pocket door." She clicked the flashlight on her cell phone and stepped inside. Just as Billy described, fairy lights hung around the little room. She plugged them in and looked around. It was a treasure room.

Except these riches wouldn't pay Mr. Dawson's bills or help Billy out of debt. They wouldn't restore the Winslow family to its former level in society.

Big, fluffy pillows covered the floor. The only furniture was a bookshelf filled with books like *The Black Stallion*, *A Tree Grows in Brooklyn*, and *Anne of Green Gables*. An antique mirror hung on the wall. There was a picture of her mother and grandparents with a swim meet ribbon hanging off the frame. Her mom had placed first. Sara picked up a stuffed animal. A black kitten that reminded her of one she'd had as a child. They'd named him Binx. A My Little Pony, little discs with neon pictures, and a couple of music discs cluttered one shelf. She inspected each item, taking her time, as if she were a museum curator, then carefully put them back where they belonged.

On the top of the bookshelf sat a cedar box.

She scooted closer. If the brooch was there, this was where it had to be. She didn't believe it was there though. This wasn't a family's hiding place. It was a little-girl-turned-teen's refuge. These were her mother's treasures. Later her grandmother's as she held her daughter's memories tight.

Sara wanted everyone to leave, to give her time alone, to let the tears she fought flow. For a moment in time, she had her mother back. She wanted to cuddle up with her mom's stuffed animal and sleep in that little room surrounded by her mother's love.

But they were waiting.

Waiting to see if she discovered some forgotten possession that had probably been long sold or stolen.

Thad squatted down next to her. He didn't reach for her or the cedar chest. Just lent his warmth and strength. "How are you doing?"

"I'm okay." She reached for the cedar chest and lifted the lid. Inside were letters, a journal, and more mementos. "No jewelry."

Mr. Dawson's groan broke the silence. Sara pushed up off the floor, and Thad moved out of the room, giving her space again. Sara pulled the door shut, locked the door, and pocketed the key. It was her mom's space. She didn't want anyone else in there.

"I'm sorry, Mr. Dawson. Even if we'd found the brooch, I couldn't let you have it. It belongs to the royal family of the Netherlands."

"I know. You're a good person, like your mother and your grandparents. Thank you for letting me be a part of your discovery." He turned to Thad. "Go ahead and call the police. I won't resist."

Thad looked over at her, uncertainty in his eyes. His mouth pulled down, and his brows pinched at the bridge of his nose. She gave a slight shake of her head. What was the point of sending Mick Dawson to jail? Who would take care of his ailing mother? No one had gotten hurt, and he didn't actually steal anything.

"Mr. Dawson, do you truly regret your actions?" she asked.

"I was a desperate fool, but that doesn't excuse what I did. Saying I'm sorry isn't enough. Royal and Marian were my friends. I betrayed their trust in me with what I've done."

Thad laced his fingers through hers and gave a little squeeze of encouragement. "Mr. Dawson, from what I've heard, you've been a beloved member of this community for years and you've been under a lot of stress," Sara said.

"That doesn't excuse my actions."

"No, it doesn't. But what I think Sara is trying to say is, you made a mistake but not one that you can't fix."

"Exactly," Sara said. "I'm not looking to ruin your life or your reputation. I just wanted answers. Well, answers and a good night's sleep."

Mr. Dawson winced and apologized again. "I have to make up for what I've done."

"I agree, but I don't think prison is the right answer in this case. You can start by asking God's forgiveness," she said.

"I will. I promise."

"And you do community service," Thad said. "We could talk to Pastor Gary tomorrow after service. I'm sure he could use some help with the summer programs."

"Would you both come with me?" Mr. Dawson lifted his chin to look Sara in the eye. "I want to show you I'm willing to do the work to make reparations."

"Of course," she said.

Billy, who had kept silent during all of this, cleared his throat. "I know of a good financial guy who might be of some help."

Thad glanced at her, but she squeezed his hand, hoping he'd keep quiet.

Billy must have caught the exchange. "I haven't been honest with everyone. Not even myself. I lost my job a few months ago. I was arrogant and foolish. My wife doesn't even know. I thought I could get myself out of the mess on my own before anyone found out. Then I had some losses at the casino, and I took out a couple of those quick loans. I was going to ask Royal for help, but he passed away before I could get up enough nerve. Now I'm behind on my mortgage, and I'm afraid that when I tell Deb, she'll leave me."

He turned to Mr. Dawson. "Desperation is something I understand. I contacted Sara because I was hoping she'd give me a loan from her inheritance. I knew Royal and Marian had a big life insurance policy and they'd named her the beneficiary. But I couldn't follow through with my plans."

"Did you try to break in here too, for the brooch?" Sara asked.

"No, I didn't."

"And your story about being in New York for work?"

"It's true. I went to this finance guy a few days ago, and he's actually the one who got me the interview. A friend of a friend thing. My interview was in New York, but I'll be starting at the Hartford office on Monday. Hopefully, when I tell Deb about the new job, she'll forgive me for the lies I told."

"So now what?" Mr. Dawson asked.

Thad smiled at him. "You go home, and we'll see you tomorrow at church. And Billy goes home and tells his wife the truth."

Sara walked the group to the front door, her steps heavy with exhaustion. It had been a long week in Hazardville. After Mr. Dawson and Billy left, Thad turned to her.

"Want to talk about everything?"

She thought about it. About the break-ins and Mr. Dawson's confession as well as her cousin's, and she thought about that little room at the top of the house calling her name. Did she want to dissect everything? No, she didn't, at least not right now. She had a lot to process, including how she felt about the man in front of her and their relationship going forward.

"It's late, but thank you for being here. Let's talk tomorrow."

∼ CHAPTER THIRTEEN ∼

Sara overslept on Sunday and missed church. After everyone left the night before she locked up the house, set the alarm, and climbed the stairs to the top floor. She unlocked the little tower room, picked up the toy kitten, and fell asleep on the multitude of pillows.

She dreamed of her mom and woke up with a light in her heart. She felt a peace about her decision not to press charges against Mick Dawson. Sending him to prison wouldn't help anyone. A desperate man who had devoted his life to helping others, first as a teacher, then as a coach and a good son, would have had his life ruined. Her mother would have hated that. She had a feeling her grandparents would have too.

But she had decisions to make. She'd asked for guidance, but the answer was slow in coming. Instead of sitting at home this morning, she'd hopped into her car and driven around town with no particular destination in mind. By the time she returned home, she had the answers she'd been seeking.

Thad's truck rumbled into her driveway, and she headed out to the porch to meet him. She'd sent him a text asking him to handle the meeting between Mr. Dawson and the pastor. Butterflies twisted and turned, dancing inside of her. She hadn't been this nervous ever with Thad, but things were different now.

"How did it go at church?" she asked.

"Mr. Dawson confessed everything to Pastor Gary, and they're working out a schedule and a way for him to make it right. Pastor Gary knows of a few organizations that can help with Mrs. Dawson's medical bills."

Sara took a step backward to keep herself from throwing her arms around Thad. She didn't want to make him spill the coffee or drop the bag he carried. Plus, they needed to talk. "Thank you for taking care of that for me."

"You're welcome. This is for you." He handed her a coffee and the brown bag. "Scones. Julie made strawberry with cream this time."

"Have I told you that your sister is an amazing person?"

"No, but I agree, and so are you. Most people wouldn't have forgiven Mick Dawson for his actions."

"If nothing else, moving here has taught me an important lesson." She sat down on the top step and patted the spot next to her. "People make mistakes, but those mistakes shouldn't define you. They shouldn't rule your life."

"It was still wrong," Thad said.

"Oh, I'm not arguing that point. It was clear he was remorseful, and had he not been too stubborn to seek help, we could have avoided this whole mess. Now he has to live with his regrets, just like my grandfather and my mom. They both made mistakes, but the biggest one was in not forgiving each other. They lost out on so much. Love is about forgiving each other when you mess up. So I choose to forgive Mick Dawson. I want love to rule my life, not regret."

Thad's chest constricted as he listened to Sara's declaration. Did that mean she forgave him too? Did he still have a chance? Julie had told him to go big, to make a grand gesture to show Sara how he felt. He wasn't sure what even qualified as a grand gesture, but he was going to give it his all.

"In the end, I think that was your grandfather's biggest regret. He didn't come out and say it, but he told me several times to never let anything come between me and those I loved. I also think Royal and Marian would be proud of you."

"Thanks. That means a lot."

For a few minutes they sat in silence on the front steps as kids whizzed by on their bikes, the birds chirped nearby, and Sara nibbled on her scone and drank her beloved coffee. He'd tried to eat a scone, but it stuck in his throat. He set it aside, along with his coffee, and turned to Sara. Before he could speak, nails skittered across the wood floor as an animal ran straight for him.

"Sara, why is there a pony on your porch?"

She laughed and petted the beast. "This is Duke von Milliken. He's a Great Dane puppy."

Thad eyed the dog, who must have weighed a good seventy-five pounds. The dog sniffed him then flopped into his lap.

Sara reached over and picked up a little gray and white bundle of fur. "This is his best friend, Lady Daphne, and trust me when I say she's the one in charge."

"You adopted a dog *and* a cat?"

"You know what they say. Go big or go home." She shrugged and grinned down at the fluff of fur in her lap. "They're a bonded pair. I couldn't break them up."

As she said, time to go big. "Do you think a person can fall in love in a week?" He was proud his voice came out strong and steady and didn't give away his racing heart.

"My parents knew at the end of their first date that they were meant to be together forever."

He nodded. His heart pounded louder, drowning out the birds. "If you're set on going back to Washington, I want to come with you. Sara, I knew when I heard you singing Christmas carols in June that you were the one for me. I love your sense of adventure, your strength, and your gentle heart. I love you."

Her eyes grew wide as she sat up straight.

"You love me?"

"I do, very much."

Sara set her now-empty coffee cup down and took his hand. "I'm not leaving."

"Are you sure? I can be a handyman anywhere. I just want you to be happy."

She glanced around at the yard and the pets, and then her eyes met his. "I came to Connecticut for an adventure and a chance to start over. I definitely got an adventure, but I found so much more. I found a home and a purpose and love."

She placed her hand on his cheek. "I love you too."

He bent his head and captured her lips. Relief and happiness coursed through him. He'd found his true love. He wanted to shout to the world that Sara Loomis loved him.

She grinned at him. "I also figured out a few other things."

"Such as?"

"What I should be doing with my life…besides happily dating you."

"Are you going to go ahead with the bed-and-breakfast idea?"

Sara shook her head, the happy smile slipping a little. "After the past two weeks, I'm not ready to invite strangers into my home."

"I think that's understandable. So what then? Interior design?"

"Well, when I was at the shelter this morning, I got to talking with the director. They're expecting a transfer of animals from another shelter down south. She's worried about getting all of them adopted quickly. Summer is a slow time for them because so many people are traveling for vacation."

Thad looked at the sleeping animals. "Are you planning to open your own shelter?"

Sara laughed. "Hotel Loomis, the best pet hotel in New England? It has a nice ring to it, but no. One of my former jobs in Washington included handling all of the company's social media. So I pitched her this idea, and tomorrow I start as their social media maven."

"Congratulations." Thad slipped an arm around her to pull her closer without disturbing the pets. "They're lucky to have you, as am I."

"Would you really have moved to Washington for me?"

"In a heartbeat. Your grandmother told me when I found the one, that I'd know. She was right. It doesn't matter to me if we're here or there, or somewhere else. As long as you're in my life, that's what matters the most."

She gave him that smile that lit up his world. "My grandmother was a wise woman. I knew the first time you smiled at me you were special. The way you help everyone, how you care about everyone around you? I love that. I love you."

Thad grinned back at her. "And what about the brooch? Do you think it's in the house somewhere?"

She shrugged. "Who knows? We've got the rest of our lives to find out."

He leaned in to kiss her again.

Duke took that opportunity to lick his chin, giving his approval. Thad and Sara pulled apart, both laughing. Thad scratched the kitten behind the ear, earning him the loudest purr he'd ever heard. He looked at the two pets and the woman he loved. It was crazy to think that just over a week ago, he'd been alone and a little lost. He hadn't even known what was missing in his life until he'd looked into a pair of eyes that radiated so much joy his world had lit up.

"Life together, with you," he said, "is going to be the greatest adventure I could dream of."

Dear Reader,

We are excited to bring you these stories of love, loss, and forgiveness. Gail and I have been friends for a long time. We met at our local writers' group meeting when we were baby writers starting to learn our craft. We were thrilled to be able to team up to write these stories.

Our inspiration came from an old Victorian house just across the street from my own. The house was built in 1890, and every time I walk past it, I wonder about the history of the original owner. What was their story? What did the house look like when it was brand-new? What secrets are hidden in its many rooms?

I showed the house to Gail, and our curiosities bloomed into these stories. We sincerely hope you enjoy our work.

Sincerely,
Bethany and Gail

About the Authors

Bethany John

Bethany John is a writer and schoolteacher who currently resides in an idyllic small town in western Connecticut. In her free time, she enjoys spending time at the lake and hanging out with her large extended family.

Gail Kirkpatrick

Gail Kirkpatrick learned to read at her grandpa's knee at the age of three. Since then, she's devoured books in all genres. She loves to bake, watch funny animal videos, and watch the sunset over the Long Island Sound. As a former Navy wife, she's lived in eight states and three countries and brings that knowledge to her stories. These days she calls Connecticut home along with her amazing husband, kids, and a demanding pup.

STORY BEHIND THE NAME

Hazardville, Connecticut

In 1835, on the shores of the Scantic River in northern Connecticut, the first black-powder mill was opened by Allen Loomis. Back then the area was known as Powder Hollow. Two years later, Colonel Augustus George Hazard bought into the company. By 1843, Colonel Hazard was the sole owner and changed the mill's name to the Hazard Powder Company. It was then that the surrounding village became known as Hazardville.

The mill and the village enjoyed success and growth until 1913 when a fire destroyed the mill.

Today, Hazardville is a section of Enfield, Connecticut. A few of the powder company buildings remain, having been repurposed for other uses.

Marian Moffitt's Award-Winning Zucchini Bread

Ingredients:

2 cups sugar

1 cup oil

3 eggs

2 teaspoons vanilla extract

3 cups flour

1 tablespoon cinnamon

1 teaspoon baking soda

1 teaspoon salt

½ teaspoon baking powder

3 cups grated zucchini, packed tight

½ cup nuts, chopped (optional)

1 cup raisins (optional)

1 small can crushed pineapple, drained

Directions:

Grease two 8×4-inch loaf pans and dust with flour.

Beat sugar and oil until well blended. Add eggs and vanilla extract. Beat until blended.

In a large bowl, mix dry ingredients.

Add sifted dry ingredients to wet, alternating with zucchini. Stir well. Stir in raisins, nuts, and pineapple.

Pour into loaf pans. Bake at 300 degrees for one hour. Done when toothpick inserted in the middle comes out clean. Cool 15 minutes in pan then remove to rack for cooling.

Enjoy!

Read on for a sneak peek of another exciting book
in the Love's a Mystery series!

Love's a Mystery *in*
Deadwood, Oregon
by Emily Quinn & Laura Bradford

Love Is an Art
By Emily Quinn

On the Road to Portland, Oregon
1950

Roberta Stevens wiggled in the hard bus seat, trying to get comfortable. She'd spent the last six hours staring out the window, wondering how she could have been so wrong. Not only was she not Mrs. Philip Collins today, but the man she'd given her heart to had left town with the money they'd been gifted by friends and family to start their new life together. All she had left was thirty dollars and this bus ticket to Portland, Oregon. Thank goodness Mama always preached that Roberta should keep some pin money on her. When she'd bought the ticket in St. Louis, the ticket agent had looked at her like she was insane. Now, watching the miles go past, one field at a time, she was starting to agree with his assessment. She still had her pride, but what did that do for her in this situation?

Roberta pulled up the edges of her now not-so-white gloves as she considered her situation. One thing she knew for certain. She couldn't have stayed in St. Louis. Every time her friends looked at her, she'd know what they were thinking. *Poor Roberta, she was clueless.* She touched the neckline of her shirt and felt Grandma's pearls around her neck. Those pearls and the engagement ring that she still wore were her reserves. The ring she would sell as soon as she arrived in Portland, providing it was worth anything. Since Philip had tried to get her to give it to him the night before their wedding, saying he wanted to get it attached to the wedding ring before the ceremony, it probably was worth something. At least enough to get her settled. Even if it was in a rented room while she looked for work.

When he didn't show up at the church on their wedding day, at first she thought he was angry about her refusal to give him the ring. Then her friend's husband went to the boardinghouse, and Philip's room was empty. Instead of standing at the altar, waiting for her, he was gone. Along with all his belongings and the gifts that people had given them before the wedding. When she realized that he wasn't going to show, she thanked everyone for coming and asked them to take the presents they'd brought back home with them. There would be no need for a new set of linens or even the quilt her grandmother had made for Roberta's wedding bed. She had no groom.

Roberta blinked away tears as she smoothed a wrinkle out of her skirt. The saleswoman had assured her that the fabric was perfect for traveling and wouldn't wrinkle during the long drive to their

Florida honeymoon and a new life. She'd been wrong. Everything was wrong. Moving and starting over had been Philip's idea. Philip's plans. He was probably already in Florida. Sitting on the beach he'd promised her with a cold drink in his hand.

Now, thinking of a drink made her thirsty. But the mason jar she'd brought from her apartment and refilled with water at the last stop was already empty. The bus driver talked about making good time and limiting the stops they made, so she didn't know when she'd be able to refill it.

A bottle of orange soda came into view from her left. She turned and saw that the seat next to her had been taken by a large man in a black suit. He wore a fedora and carried a tan case, much like her own that she had slid under the seat. "Excuse me, miss," he said, holding out the bottle, "but you look thirsty. It's awfully dry and hot on this bus."

She forced a smile. Just because she was out of sorts didn't mean she should be rude. "I don't want to take your soda."

"You're not taking if I give it to you freely." He smiled kindly at her. "Besides, I'm only doing my Christian duty. I can't let a fellow traveler thirst next to me when I bought two sodas at our last stop."

Roberta reached to take it, but then she paused. "I'm afraid I don't know your name."

He took his hat off, and Roberta noticed the thin comb-over of brown hair on the top of his head. He reminded her of her father. He took a handkerchief out of his suit pocket and wiped the sweat from his brow. "Robert Smith. But please, call me Bob."

"Well, we have something in common. Were you named after your father?" Roberta stared at the man sitting next to her as she accepted the opened soda. She took a sip, and the sugary orange taste brightened her mood. What was it about a treat that made one instantly feel better about the world? "Thank you for the soda. You were right, it's just what I needed."

"I *was* named after my father. How did you know? He would have been very proud, since now his name is part of the United States Postal Service. I have my commission papers right here." He dug into his case and showed her a letter of introduction from the United States Postal Service. He pointed to the name on the letter. "See? Robert Nelson Smith. The new postmaster of Deadwood, Oregon. Although, I'm not so certain I'm the man for the job."

"Congratulations on the posting. I'm sure you'll be great. I was also named after my father. I'm Roberta Stevens." She took another small sip. The man—*Bob*—she corrected herself, not only was around her father's age, but he ran a post office. Mama would have said he was bona fide with those credentials and safe to talk with. But then again, her mother had loved Philip from the start as well. Maybe no one in Roberta's family had good taste in men. "I appreciate the soda. I'll buy you one at the next stop."

"No need. I'm just hoping the stop will be long enough for me to take a short walk around the bus station. My legs are beginning to cramp." He glanced out the window. "I was hoping to be able to stay in St. Louis. I was courting someone, but when she heard where I was going, she wasn't interested in living in such a small town."

"I'm sorry. Did you love her?" Roberta held up her hand. "Sorry again to be so personal. I'm not sure what's gotten into me."

"It's riding the bus." He smiled, which made her relax. "You feel like you can tell your seatmate anything, since you'll probably never see them again. I'll go first. I was in love with Harriet, and leaving her behind has made me question even taking this job. I'm pretty sure the only reason I'm doing so is to please my parents. There, that feels better to say it out loud. Thank you for listening. What about you? What secret are you holding that you need to tell someone?"

She took a deep breath and then blurted it out. All of it. How Philip had wooed her then betrayed her and stolen their wedding money. "Now I feel like a fool. So I'm starting over. New life, new opportunities, in Portland."

"That's quite a story. You're a brave woman, Roberta Stevens. I'm proud to have met you." He yawned and tucked his case under the bench seat in front of them. "This heat is making me sleepy. Wake me when we get to the next stop, okay, Roberta?"

"Of course." Roberta went back to staring out the window. So much for having someone to talk to. It had been nice to tell someone everything. Someone who wouldn't call her naive or judge her for making poor decisions. It must be a sign that she was doing the right thing. She finished the soda, and the sound of the tires beating the road combined with the warm summer sun coming in the window to lull her into sleep as well.

When she woke, she was alone on the bus. She checked her earrings to see if they'd fallen off while she slept. They were still there. As was the ring and the pearls, and she saw her case under the seat. The driver had stopped the bus at a way station. She ran into him as she went down the aisle and exited the bus.

"You only have ten minutes, so I suggest you speed up if you don't want to be left behind in Nebraska." He was eating a sandwich, and Roberta's stomach growled at the smell. He grinned. "Food's at the far end of the station by the restrooms. I'll wait for you, but hurry."

She rushed toward the station door. She needed to find the ladies' room, fill her water jar, and buy the cheapest sandwich she could find plus a soda for Mr. Smith.

Eleven minutes later, her list complete, she climbed back onto the bus. "I made it!" Out of breath, she grinned at the driver.

"You're lucky I'm a good guy." He glanced at his watch then looked up at her and matched her grin. "I'm just teasing you. We're still missing a passenger. I couldn't have left anyway. Go find your seat, and I'll see what's keeping the other guy."

She moved though row after row of shoulders, trying not to step on anyone's foot. No one even looked up as she passed by. She'd been right in her first decision as an unengaged woman. Escaping St. Louis was the best way to forget about Philip and the life he'd promised she'd be living right now.

Her row was empty. Bob Smith must be the missing passenger.

She slid into the window seat and looked around to see if Mr. Smith had changed seats. No, he wasn't on the bus. She watched out the window as a police officer came up to the driver outside the station. They talked for a few minutes, and then the driver got back on the bus.

"We're on our way to Portland. Settle in and get some sleep while I take care of the driving," he announced over the intercom.

Roberta hurried up front. "The man who was sitting next to me isn't on the bus," she said to the driver.

"Did you know him?"

Roberta shook her head. "No. We talked for a few minutes, but I didn't know him."

The driver nodded at the station where the police officer had disappeared inside. "I'm sorry, but no one can find him. We can't wait forever. The officer has his information, so we'll get him on the next bus when he shows up."

"Oh my goodness." Roberta nervously looked around the now empty parking lot. "He said he wanted to stretch his legs."

"He knew how long we were going to be here. I told everyone who got off the bus. Miss, you need to get in your seat. We've got to get this bus going so we're not late pulling into our next stop." He started the engine and turned away from her.

Roberta retreated down the aisle. Now people were watching her, wondering why she was delaying their trip. She sank into her seat and studied the gathering night. She couldn't see anyone near the building. Maybe they'd find Mr. Smith walking down the road. It really wasn't her concern, but she had wanted to repay him for the soda.

After she finished eating and they'd gone miles past the way station, she decided to pull out her drawing pad and focus on the sunset they were driving into rather than the nice man who'd missed the bus. She picked up her case and pulled out a leather folder. *What in the world?* She didn't have a leather folder. She opened the case wider and realized her pad was gone. As were her drawing pencils.

She glanced around the seats, but most people were asleep. Who would steal papers and pencils anyway? She opened the leather folder and realized it was the commission paperwork for the Deadwood Post Office. She had Bob Smith's case. The gold engraving on the outside said *RS.* Just like hers did. She bent down to look under the seats and used her foot to check for another case. Nothing.

Her case was gone. All of her art supplies—her colored pencils, her notebook, her brushes—gone. And she had Mr. Smith's case instead. She put the commission back into the folder and put the case under the seat. Nothing was going her way today.

Tears began to blur her eyes. She tried to will them away. She could buy more art supplies when she got settled. Crying over Philip's betrayal would be fruitless. She let her emotions settle, and then she checked the map they'd given her when she bought the ticket. They would stop in Deadwood on their way to Portland. She'd just get off, leave the case and the commission with the sheriff, then be on her way. It was the right thing to do.

She wiped the tears from her face and took off her jacket to use as a blanket. Tomorrow would be better. It had to be.

Jonathan Devons nodded to his foreman, Roland Farmer, as he left the lumber mill for the night. *A good day's work,* Roland had called out to the crew as they finished cutting the last log into boards. Jonathan knew it was a dangerous day's work as well, but after the money he'd brought with him had run out, he needed a job. Deadwood wasn't a busy metropolis like Chicago, where he'd come from. He'd been lucky to find a job at all. Roland was kin to the woman who ran the boardinghouse where he'd gotten a room, and she'd taken a shine to him, as his mother would say. Jonathan thought the shine was more for her daughter, who didn't look old enough to be out of school, much less looking for a husband.

But things worked differently here. Or maybe they worked like this everywhere and Jonathan had never noticed. He'd been betrothed to one woman since his college graduation. Now that was over, and he was apparently back on the market, whether he wanted to be or not. He took his cap off and brushed the sawdust out of his hair. He'd need to get it cut sooner rather than later, as he was looking a little ragged. Even for someone who worked with his hands and not at the corporate offices he'd left behind in Chicago.

He dodged a car that had turned onto the only paved street in town. Deadwood was on the highway that went north to Portland and south to Eugene. He hadn't decided which way he'd go when he left, but he wanted to get to the coast and see the ocean before he settled down anywhere. Seeing the car reminded him of his own sedan, sitting outside the boardinghouse like a yard ornament. There wasn't much of a reason to drive the few blocks to the lumber mill every morning. He saw his car as his own magic carpet, like in the Aladdin stories. Just waiting to take him to his next adventure.

Instead of heading directly to the boardinghouse and his room to wash up and wait for dinner, he turned toward the town square, which was a park with a fountain in the middle and a few benches scattered around it. The city offices and the general store surrounded the park as did the just-completed post office and another building that soon would be a new library if the town got a Carnegie grant. The building that currently held the town's small book collection was off the park, not grand enough for the current town fathers to provide funding or a proper building.

Or at least that was his take on the discussions occurring at work and at the dinner table. He tried to stay out of Deadwood politics, but Mrs. Elliott liked her guests to be current on the local gossip. Especially when they were here for more than a week, like Jonathan had been. He'd had enough of politics at his father's dinner table to last a lifetime. Maybe parents and children always came down on the opposite side of the events of the day. At least he had. His brother hadn't cared one way or another.

Jonathan leaned back on the white park bench, watching the town around him. He always said that writers were like magpies—they picked up little bits and pieces everywhere and used them in their books. His book. He rubbed his face. He hadn't worked on his novel for days. Okay, maybe it had been weeks. He'd left the typewriter at home. It was too bulky to pack with him on what the Australians would call a walkabout. His journal would have to do. However, all he'd been writing in the journal lately were his days' activities.

The last few entries had looked the same. Seven a.m. wake up. Coffee and breakfast at the boardinghouse. Then to work, where he took trees cut down in the forest and made them into boards. Boards for new houses and barns. Boards for new stores and the new post office. Deadwood was booming and needed a lot of boards. After work, he'd come here to the park and sit for a while so the muse could visit. And when it didn't, he'd close his journal and tuck it into his pocket. Then go to dinner at the boardinghouse, while away a couple of hours, and fall asleep while trying to read in the dim light in his room.

And the next day he'd do the same.

Even his muse was bored.

Maybe the idea of a novel was presumptuous. His professors had warned him that the publishing industry was a hard life. They'd tried to steer him toward editing or accounting, where he could work in the book world and still eat, if not earn enough to have a family.

He'd tried to explain this to his father the day he'd graduated, but Father had told Jonathan what his future was going to be. He was joining the family construction business and marrying a proper match. Since Jonathan hadn't found a suitable wife during his college years, the family had a solution. No muss, no fuss. Everything was settled.

Except Jonathan hadn't wanted the life his father had set up for him, including the ready-made wife. And now, he was reliving the same day over and over. Paying penance for leaving Chicago? For rejecting the life he'd been given? Or was this just the way life worked?

Either way, Jonathan needed a change. He mentally calculated how much money he had set aside not counting his trust. He didn't have quite enough to get him to a bigger town, but he was getting close. Maybe next week he'd pack up the sedan and leave. Three weeks at the max. That would give time for the parcel he was waiting for to arrive. Once the new journal came, he'd start working on his book. He was sure of it. There was nothing like a new journal to get the juices flowing.

He closed his eyes and listened to the birds chirping. Now that he had a plan in place, things didn't look so bleak. Or so boring. By fall, he'd be settled in a new job and a new life. And he could forget his old life completely. Reinvention number two?

He watched the bus coming down the street. Maybe the driver would bring mail with him. His mother would say the bus was a sign. But then, she believed in signs. He didn't. He believed in hard work. Signs led you astray.

Jonathan gathered his pen and journal and put them in his jacket pocket. Then he followed the bus to its stopping point next to the general store. *God rewards those who wait,* he thought as he lingered on the porch to see if the driver dropped off a bag of mail.

He was doing the work. Now he just needed to complete the plan. Things were looking up.

A Note from the Editors

We hope you enjoyed another volume in the Love's a Mystery series, created by Guideposts. For over seventy-five years, Guideposts, a nonprofit organization, has been driven by a vision of a world filled with hope. We aspire to be the voice of a trusted friend, a friend who makes you feel more hopeful and connected.

By making a purchase from Guideposts, you join our community in touching millions of lives, inspiring them to believe that all things are possible through faith, hope, and prayer. Your continued support allows us to provide uplifting resources to those in need. Whether through our communities, websites, apps, or publications, we inspire our audiences, bring them together, and comfort, uplift, entertain, and guide them. Visit us at guideposts.org to learn more.

We would love to hear from you. Write us at Guideposts, P.O. Box 5815, Harlan, Iowa 51593 or call us at (800) 932-2145. Did you love *Love's a Mystery in Hazardwille, Connecticut*? Leave a review for this product on guideposts.org/shop. Your feedback helps others in our community find relevant products.

Find inspiration, find faith, find Guideposts.

Shop our best sellers and favorites at
guideposts.org/shop

Or scan the QR code to go directly to our Shop

Find more inspiring stories in these best-loved Guideposts fiction series!

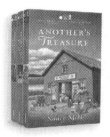

Mysteries of Lancaster County

Follow the Classen sisters as they unravel clues and uncover hidden secrets in Mysteries of Lancaster County. As you get to know these women and their friends, you'll see how God brings each of them together for a fresh start in life.

Secrets of Wayfarers Inn

Retired schoolteachers find themselves owners of an old warehouse-turned-inn that is filled with hidden passages, buried secrets, and stunning surprises that will set them on a course to puzzling mysteries from the Underground Railroad.

Tearoom Mysteries Series

Mix one stately Victorian home, a charming lakeside town in Maine, and two adventurous cousins with a passion for tea and hospitality. Add a large scoop of intriguing mystery, and sprinkle generously with faith, family, and friends, and you have the recipe for *Tearoom Mysteries*.

Ordinary Women of the Bible

Richly imagined stories—based on facts from the Bible—have all the plot twists and suspense of a great mystery, while bringing you fascinating insights on what it was like to be a woman living in the ancient world.

To learn more about these books, visit Guideposts.org/Shop

Printed in the United States
by Baker & Taylor Publisher Services